Birdmagic

HOLLY WEBB

◼SCHOLASTIC

First published in the UK in 2010 by Scholastic Children's Books
An imprint of Scholastic Ltd
Euston House, 24 Eversholt Street
London, NW1 1DB, UK
Registered office: Westfield Road, Southam, Warwickshire, CV47 0RA

Text copyright © Holly Webb, 2010

ISBN 978 1 407 11514 6

A CIP catalogue record for this book is available
from the British Library.

Printed and bound by CPI Group (UK) Ltd, Croydon, CR0 4YY
Papers used by Scholastic Children's Books are made from
wood grown in sustainable forests.

5 7 9 10 8 6 4

www.scholastic.co.uk/zone

For Jon, Tom, Robin and William

Lottie stood in the little yard at the back of Grace's Pet Shop, staring up at the sky and wondering what to do. It was freezing, but she didn't want to go back inside just yet. She needed a little bit of time. She was used to strange things happening now, or at least, she'd thought she was. She had been living at her uncle's magical pet shop for three months. She shared her life with a gang of rowdy pink mice, a warlike hamster, and a sarcastic rat. She was also taking magic lessons from a witch. Lottie was used to strange. But her father had just appeared behind her while she was making her dog, Sofie, coffee. Her father that she'd always been told was dead, her father that she hadn't seen for the last eight years.

"Are you all right, dear Lottie?" Sofie nudged

her cheek anxiously, her bristly whiskers tickling Lottie's face. "Do you want me to tell him to go away?"

Lottie laughed, but it wasn't really very funny. "After all that time we've spent wishing for him to come back?" she asked Sofie sadly.

Sofie shook her black ears, and stared at Lottie shrewdly. "But you did not expect him to come back like this, without his memories, did you, Lottie?"

"No-oo. . ." Lottie admitted, sighing. "I thought he'd remember me – a little, anyway. I know I was only two when he left, but he didn't remember he had a daughter at all! I don't think he even knows who *he* is." She hugged Sofie, the warm, strong, smooth-furred little body filling her with love. Sofie, a black dachshund with ginger eyebrows, was Lottie's familiar. She made Lottie's magic stronger, since they had discovered their special bond and acted as another side to Lottie's character. Sofie was the bossy, know-it-all, chocolate-obsessed side.

"We ought to go back in," Lottie murmured into the sweet vanilla-smelling fur of Sofie's head.

"Mmm. . ." Sofie agreed, but neither of them moved.

At last Lottie heaved herself away from the wall. "Uncle Jack will be back soon. It's going to be really weird for him too. We can't let him just walk in and find his long-lost brother sitting at the kitchen table."

"And we have left your father alone," Sofie added gently.

Lottie flushed. "I know. . . That was mean. But I couldn't bear it any longer, Sofie; he doesn't know who I am!"

She brushed a hand across her eyes. She had dreamed of this day, this amazing moment, for weeks and weeks, ever since she had realized that her father might still be alive. He had disappeared years ago, when they had all been living at Grace's Pet Shop, with Uncle Jack, his wife and Lottie's cousin Danny. Lottie's mother had become convinced that her husband was dead, and she and Lottie had moved away, as her mum couldn't bear living there without her dad.

Lottie had been so little that she'd forgotten her life at the shop entirely. When her mother had gone to work in France, she had been furious at being dumped with Uncle Jack, and had been prepared to hate living there. But she hadn't reckoned on it being a shop full of talking animals, who weren't

3

very good at being quiet, even when they were supposed to be keeping themselves a secret. How could she not love the hilarious pink mice and her darling Sofie?

It had been a huge shock to discover that the pretty bedroom with the pink spotty curtains had been hers once before – that she too had a magical heritage, that magic danced in her blood. With Sofie as her familiar, Lottie could do incredible things – dangerous things, sometimes. But she had never had to do anything as scary as this before. How could she introduce herself to her own father?

Lottie walked slowly back into the kitchen, running her fingers round Sofie's ears, over and over again, without even knowing.

I love you. He will love you again. Don't be sad. . . Sofie said to her silently, and Lottie used the strength Sofie gave her to smile at her father.

"I'm sorry. It was just . . . a surprise to see you. I shouldn't have run off like that."

He was sitting at the table where she had left him, his hands cupped around the mug of coffee she had made. He hadn't drunk any. He was staring at Fred, the cleverest, silliest and most adventurous of the pink mice, who was about to demonstrate how he could jump over a coffee mug, really quite easily.

Her father didn't seem surprised to be having a conversation with a mouse, Lottie noticed. He might not remember who he was, but he seemed to understand animals and their magic.

"Fred, no!" Lottie squeaked, just as the little pink mouse began his run up.

However confused and ill her father looked, he had wonderful reflexes. It seemed only a second later that he was dangling Fred by the tail above the mug, the mouse's whiskers dripping coffee.

"Lottie! That was your fault! You distracted me!" Fred spat, shaking his whiskers crossly.

"Sorry. I'm sure you would have cleared it easily. I was just worried the coffee might still be hot." Lottie's father gravely offered Fred a clean handkerchief, and he buried his whiskers in it for a while, until he felt better.

"I'll make some more. . ." Lottie murmured, picking up the mug.

"My whiskers are perfectly clean, he can drink it!" Fred snapped, somewhat muffled by the handkerchief, which he was wearing like a towel. He stalked – as much as a mouse can stalk –

across the table to Lottie's father, the handkerchief now a long trailing cloak behind him. In a very dignified manner, he climbed into the pocket of Lottie's dad's yellow anorak, and pulled the handkerchief in behind him, so that he was completely hidden.

Lottie raised her eyebrows. Fred was friendly, for a mouse – mice were generally rather nervous, skittish creatures – but even he usually took a little longer to get so familiar with someone.

"Animals seem to like me," her father explained, looking at his wriggling pocket in a puzzled sort of way.

"Of course they do!" Sofie told him witheringly. "This used to be your shop, you know! You have a magical bond with animals, the whole family does."

Lottie's father stared at Sofie, and then around the kitchen, with a heartbreaking look of amazement. He clearly had no idea. Lottie nearly bolted for the yard again. How was she going to explain everything? She had got as far as telling him her name before, but she hadn't said that she was his daughter. She hadn't been able to find a good way to do that yet.

"I lived here?" he asked slowly, running his

finger down the woodgrain of the table, as though he was tasting it through his skin.

It was just then that Danny and Uncle Jack walked into the kitchen. Danny only stared, his eyes dark and round with amazement. But Uncle Jack staggered against the door frame as he saw his brother, gasping; then he hurled himself across the room to hug him.

Lottie's father sat there stiffly, looking frightened, and frowning at Danny, whom he seemed to find very confusing.

"Is that. . ." Danny muttered to Lottie.

She nodded. "But he doesn't know. He doesn't remember anything!"

Danny gulped, and stared at his newfound uncle. "He doesn't recognize Dad," he murmured doubtfully.

Uncle Jack had obviously just realized this too. He sat back on his heels, gazing at his brother. "Where have you been, Tom?" he asked quietly. "What's happened to you?" Then he turned and looked at Lottie. "Lottie. . . You know who this is?"

"I know. I dreamed of him. . ." Lottie whispered painfully.

"She – the dog – said something about my family. . ." Lottie's father said hoarsely, his eyes searching Uncle Jack's face. "Do I have one?" He glanced at Danny. "Are you them? He reminds me of someone."

Uncle Jack pulled out a chair and sat down heavily. "Danny is your nephew. My son. He looks like you did as a boy; I can see why you'd recognize him."

Danny put his arm round Lottie's shoulders, and she resisted the sudden urge to push him away. He was being nice. It wasn't his fault her dad recognized him, and not his own daughter.

"You're my brother then? I have a brother?" Lottie's dad smiled, as though he could hardly believe it.

"You really don't remember?" Uncle Jack asked.

Lottie's dad shook his head. "No. I'm sorry. . ." he said gently. "It must seem very rude of me. I can't believe I have a family again. A nephew! And a niece?" he suggested, looking at Lottie.

Lottie shook her head. She knew she and Danny looked alike, both with the dark curly hair that Uncle Jack and her dad had passed on.

Uncle Jack waited for her to say something, then realized she wasn't going to. He laid a hand on his brother's arm. "Tom, Lottie is Danny's cousin. Your daughter."

Lottie's father gaped at her, like someone in a cartoon, with his mouth hanging open. She could practically see the question marks floating above his head.

"I have a child?" he whispered. "A girl. . ." He gazed at Lottie, staring and staring, as though he was trying to fix every detail in his mind. Then he ducked his head shyly before looking up, this time meeting Lottie's eyes. "How old are you?" he asked, quietly, as though it hurt him as much to have to ask as it hurt her that he didn't already know.

"I'm nearly eleven," Lottie muttered.

Her father stood up, and came towards her.

Lottie clutched Sofie even more tightly. She felt like backing away towards the wall, but she couldn't. She was frozen. He just didn't feel like her father, that was the problem. She had wanted him to sweep her into his arms and hug her till she couldn't breathe. She had wanted him to tell her that he had missed her and her mother desperately every minute. She had wanted him to explain that he had been imprisoned by an evil enchantress for the last eight years, and hadn't been able to twitch his eyebrows, let alone escape and come rushing back to her. But he hadn't. And now she wasn't ready for him.

She didn't want this strange, hesitant, almost frightened man. Even if he did look exactly like the photos she'd treasured for so long. And she could see that she'd inherited his long, soot-black eyelashes. Spiders' legs, her mum always called them to tease her. *Mum!* She hadn't thought of how this was going to be for her mother too. Her husband back, after all this time, but with no memory of their time together. Lottie bit into her bottom lip. She couldn't deal with that as well right now.

Sofie nudged Lottie under the chin, and then wriggled out of her arms, leaping athletically at her dad.

Lottie's dad caught Sofie automatically, and gasped.

"I am not that heavy," Sofie told him sternly, and he looked apologetic. "Lottie feeds me too much chocolate." Sofie gave a mournful sigh, and Danny sniggered.

Lottie was hardly listening. She was too surprised. Sofie was her familiar, and they shared their thoughts and feelings so much of the time that she usually knew what Sofie was planning. But that jump had been a shock.

Obviously Sofie trusted her dad. Even if she didn't.

Lottie, I know this is hard, but he is a good person. I can smell him. Sofie's message wrapped round her mind like chocolate silk, and Lottie sighed. She took a step towards her father, and stroked Sofie's velvet head with him, so that their hands touched.

His hand was cold, from nerves perhaps, as well as from being out in the chilly winter afternoon. But she could feel the quiver of the magic under his skin, and it felt familiar, like her own. She supposed it was – after all, the magic in her blood had been passed on from him.

It was rather like the feeling she got from Sofie – that they were bound together by magic.

Right now she could sense his confused happiness as he laid his hand over hers. He had nice, big hands, she noticed. Very worn and rough, but comforting.

Lottie glanced up at him cautiously, and met an answering look coming back. A slightly suspicious, watchful, one-raised-black-eyebrow look. She gave a little gasp of a laugh, and her father chuckled. Slowly, as though he thought she might push him away, he put one arm round her, squidging Sofie in between them.

"I'm sorry," he told her gently. "I can see I'm . . . a disappointment."

Lottie started to shake her head reassuringly, and realized that was silly. Why tell polite little lies? He knew how she felt anyway, it seemed.

"I'll get it back. My memory, I mean. I'm sure I will. There are some things about this place, they feel as though they're floating about somewhere just outside my head. And if – *when* – those memories float close enough, I'll snatch them back." He nodded. "I promise." Then he muttered something that Lottie only just caught. "How many years of you have I missed. . ."

Lottie could feel that he didn't really want an answer yet. She managed to smile, her eyes burning with half-happy tears, and she hugged him back. It felt nice but odd. A bit like hugging one of her mother's friends, someone she was supposed to remember, who said they remembered her. Except her father didn't remember her at all.

"Mmmpf. Good. Now you are both being sensible, *get off me!*" Sofie yapped, wriggling furiously out of their arms and taking a dangerous leap on to the kitchen table, where she sat, panting furiously to get her breath back. "What do you think I am, a stuffed toy?"

"You might talk more sense if you were," a

grumpy voice muttered from somewhere round their feet, and Lottie jumped. "Back then, are we, Tom? About time. Never wrote. Not even so much as a postcard. No manners."

Horace, the African grey parrot, hardly ever left his perch in the shop window, but he had apparently decided to make an exception for today. He made a clumsy, fluttering leap – he was old, and his wings were stiff – and scrambled up to a chair, and then on to the table next to Sofie. She twitched her whiskers at him haughtily, but didn't answer back. All the animals in the shop were half-afraid of Horace – he had been there for ever, and yet there was something strangely unfamiliar about him. He was the only creature who could speak to the customers when they weren't magical people but everyday folk after dog biscuits or hamster bedding. He had to keep himself to nursery rhymes and rude words, mostly, but occasionally he would say something meaningful, and then gaze back at them slyly with his yellow eyes when they looked up at him in shock.

Now his yellow eyes were fixed mockingly on Sofie. "Cat got your tongue?" he suggested, and Sofie hissed with disgust. She hated cats, and she had been cruelly tormented by the litter of black kittens who lived in the back room of the shop.

"Sweet-natured as ever, old Firebird," Lottie's father murmured, running a loving hand over Horace's soft grey feathers.

Everyone else gasped. Horace hadn't bitten his fingers off, and Lottie's dad seemed to know who Horace was, even if he called him something different.

"You recognize him then?" Uncle Jack asked anxiously, watching Horace sidle across the table, crooning quietly to himself in pleasure as his old owner ruffled his feathers.

Lottie's father blinked, and then looked down at Horace as though he had bitten him after all. "Yes. Yes, I do. I do remember. I know you." He smiled, taking in a shaky breath of relief. "I remember. . ."

Lottie looked helplessly at the parrot, who was flicking his red tail feathers back and forth as he eyed his audience. He stared back, then fluttered off the table and swooped gracefully on to her shoulder, where he nibbled her earlobe gently. Lottie froze. Horace had never done anything like this before, and she wasn't sure how good his eyesight was these days. If she moved he might have her ear off, without even meaning to. Or at least, he'd *say* he hadn't meant to. . .

"Be brave, you silly girl," the parrot muttered in her ear. "Just remember, he knew me for fifteen years before he left. You only for two. It means nothing. We'll bring his memories back."

"Why did he call you Firebird?" Lottie murmured, still shocked by Horace saying anything to her that wasn't criticism of her homework.

"I am a firebird. A phoenix. Spell it!"

Lottie's spelling had improved enormously since the stern old parrot had taken charge of her spelling lists, but Mrs Taylor had never set them that one.

"Um. F? F-E-E— "

"PH! PH!" Horace screamed, dancing up and down on her shoulder. "P-H-O-E-N-I-X!" He ruffled his feathers irritably, so he looked like a furious feather duster.

"I won't forget," Lottie promised. Then she realized what Horace had actually said. "*You're* a phoenix? I thought you were a parrot!"

"I am a parrot."

"But you said. . ."

Horace sighed, as though he thought she was

15

being very slow. "I am a phoenix currently incognito." He glared at her. "And if your excuse for a school taught anything other than bad poetry and the gory bits about the Egyptians, you would know what that meant. I'm in disguise."

"Phoenixes can choose what they look like, Lottie," Uncle Jack explained. "Horace has been a parrot for years. I'd almost forgotten what you really were," he added, grinning.

Horace snorted grumpily, and suddenly his scarlet tail feathers erupted into a mass of sparkling flames, crimson and pink and gold. Everyone took a step back, and Lottie squeaked, wondering if he was going to set her hair on fire.

"All right, sorry!" Uncle Jack said in his best soothing voice, which he usually only had to use on hysterical mice. "I know really. It's just that I'd started to think of you as a parrot. You haven't changed since. . ." He tailed off.

"Not since he left, no," Horace snapped. "Lost the enthusiasm, somehow," he added, muttering. He let his tail feathers die back to their usual scarlet, and gently pulled Lottie's hair. Then he looked over at her father, ducking his head and stamping his feet nervously. Lottie could feel his claws shifting about on her shoulder.

Tom came closer, holding out an arm for Horace to step on to, and the parrot shuffled shyly over, nuzzling against Tom's cheek.

Lottie watched in amazement. She had never seen Horace be so affectionate. To anyone. Lottie bit her lip and looked over at Danny, wondering how he was taking this.

Danny gave her an uncertain grin – he probably thought she was about to burst into tears.

"A phoenix, huh?" he muttered. It was a safer subject than Lottie suddenly having her dad back. She knew that it had been hard for Danny, when she'd told him she was sure her dad was still alive. His mum had died when he was seven. Only having one parent had been one of the few things Lottie and Danny had in common – that and knowing about a shop full of magical animals.

"Mmm. What else do phoenixes do? I can't remember." Lottie frowned, watching her dad murmur lovingly to Horace. She wasn't sure whether to wish he'd do that to her, or be glad that he wasn't. She needed some time to get used to him.

"It is unnatural, all that fiery feather business. Nasty show-off birds," Sofie hissed, but only so Lottie and Danny could hear. She hated anyone getting more attention than her.

"Do phoenixes do wishes?" Danny whispered. "Or is that sphinxes?"

"Sphinxes don't exist!" Lottie stared at him. "Do they?"

Danny shrugged. "Did you think there was a phoenix in the shop window all this time?"

"Phoenixes are reborn in fire," Sofie said in a low growl. "And they can grant wishes if they drop a feather to you."

"And they look like moth-eaten old parrots," Danny snorted, giggling rather too loudly.

Horace's head snapped up. Lottie's father's arrival seemed to have given him a new lease of life. He glared at Danny, and then he seemed to shimmer all over. His yellow eyes grew suddenly wider and rounder, staring hypnotically at Lottie and Danny. Then the shimmering cloud of light died away, and instead of an ancient and somewhat moth-eaten parrot, there was an enormous owl sitting on Tom's arm.

Danny gulped. The owl's beak was black, and very sharp-looking, but it was the saucer eyes that enthralled the children.

I bet that's how he looks at his food... Lottie thought, her heart thumping. Only Sofie's stubborn fearlessness was holding her still. Something deep inside her was screaming, *Run, run, run!*

Danny swallowed. They could catch each other's thoughts sometimes, some strange tie of being cousins, and he darted a worried glance at her.

"I don't think he's going to be happy with sunflower seeds any more. . ."

2

Uncle Jack looked worriedly at Horace, who was sitting regally on Lottie's dad's arm, staring around the shop as though it seemed different.

Lottie's dad scratched Horace's ear tufts, and Horace sank his head down even further and closed his eyes blissfully. Then he snapped them open again at once, looking surprised. "That's what it is," he murmured. "I'd forgotten how good owl sight can be." Horace glared at the kitchen cupboard. "Did you know there's a spider under there?" he asked Uncle Jack.

Lottie flinched, and Sofie gave a disgusted sniff. Neither of them liked spiders.

It was at that point that Fred the mouse decided to stop sulking, and climbed out of Lottie's dad's coat pocket.

Completely unaware of the enormous bird of prey about a metre away from him, Fred stomped across the kitchen table towards Lottie with a stubborn look about his whiskers.

"Are you going to apologize?" he snapped, flicking his tail over his arm in an aggressive sort of way.

"Fred!" Lottie yelped.

"Yes! It's me! The one you were extremely rude to. I'm not poisonous, you know. My whiskers are not going to sully a cup of coffee. Mice are not unclean. All the time. So. Have you decided to say sorry?"

"No! Fred, look—"

"Fine!" Fred's whiskers were wobbling tragically now. "I was mistaken in you, Lottie Grace, I understand that at last. I never thought I'd hear you say something quite so, so *mouse-ist!*" He turned round in a grand tail-swirling huff, but then his emotions got the better of him – pink mice were even more emotional than the normal kind – and he made for the edge of the table with his head hanging and his tail trailing out behind him.

"I didn't mean it like that – oh, Fred, be careful! Horace, no!"

21

Fred suddenly shot across the table, his mouse instincts kicking in at last. He was a pampered pet-shop creature who'd never been hunted, but there was obviously something unmistakably threatening about the swish of enormous wings as Horace launched himself through the air.

Lottie flung herself after Fred, and Sofie went with her, skidding across the table, seizing him in her jaws and diving to the floor. Lottie hit the ground on top of them both as Horace skimmed by with a harsh owl's scream, and landed on the dresser, his eyes flashing and furious.

"Wow!" Danny crouched down to pull her up. "I don't suppose you could do that again so I could film it, could you? We could make a fortune."

Lottie ignored him. "Sofie, are you all right? Oh, no, you're bleeding!"

"That stupid *hibou*, he clawed me on the way past!" Words obviously failed her after that, and Sofie let off a volley of angry barks at Horace, who sat next to a vase of flowers and hissed irritably. He did look slightly ashamed of himself.

"Typical!" Fred dragged his tail from between Sofie's teeth, and moaned lovingly over it. "She assaults me, and you ask her if *she* is all right! Just

22

look at my tail, look at it! It's all wet! She slobbered on my tail!"

"Excuse me! I do not slobber!" Sofie stopped nursing her scratched paw and glared at Fred.

Lottie scooped Fred up in one hand, trying hard to think loving, reassuring thoughts, which was very difficult while she was torn between desperately wanting to smack a large owl round the head and needing to laugh till she was sick.

"Fred, please try to calm down. Sofie didn't attack you – look, she was rescuing you. Honestly. Didn't you see Horace? He was trying to eat you!" Lottie realized just as she said it that this might not be a good idea. If anything was going to throw Fred into hysterics, that would.

But Fred stood up on her palm, ten centimetres of outraged furry dignity, and folded his paws and his tail together. "Really. Horace. The parrot. Of all the dreadful excuses. Lottie, you should be ashamed."

"But he's not a parrot he's an owl, look. . . Oh." Lottie stopped, because Horace wasn't an owl any more. He was a grey parrot with red tail feathers, and a glint in his eye which ought to have been guilt, but was probably him trying not to laugh.

"An owl!" Poor Fred was almost in tears as

he climbed down Lottie's arm, making for her dad's pocket again. "You're doing this on purpose. I don't know how you can be so cruel, Lottie!" He ran across the table, not seeing Horace twitch as some lingering owl senses fought with his parrot shape, and dived into the yellow oilskin coat. "I want the handkerchief again, I need to hide from the world," he added in a muffled squeak, and Lottie's dad helpfully pushed it in after him.

Everyone took a deep breath, and Uncle Jack sighed and put the kettle on.

"I need a cake," Sofie whimpered, holding out her paw, which was only very slightly scratched. "I am bleeding, you see?"

Uncle Jack didn't even bother to argue, he just opened the cupboard.

"What is there?" Sofie brightened up immediately. "Is there gateau? I need chocolate gateau!" She paused and sighed, as if assessing her chances here. "Profiteroles? One *leetle* profiterole? A madeleine, even. . ."

Uncle Jack shrugged. "Chocolate mini rolls. . ."

Sofie rolled her eyes to heaven. Obviously chocolate mini rolls were not sufficient for the kind of emotional trauma she had undergone. "I will need at least three," she told Uncle Jack, fixing him with a steely glare.

"Two!" Danny snapped. "There's only six in the box."

"He might not want one!" Sofie nodded elegantly at Lottie's dad, and then limped tragically over to him, lifting deep, sad, dark-brown eyes up to his face. "You can see that I need chocolate, mmm? Much more than you do?"

Lottie's dad stared down at her thoughtfully. "I think I rather like chocolate," he told her apologetically. "You told me Lottie fed you too much of it. And I have had an eventful afternoon too, you know."

Sofie scowled and stomped over to Lottie to try the eyes on her.

"Uh-uh. I definitely need mine. You're already getting two! Don't be a pig, Sofie." Lottie picked her up, and got the full force of the quivering whiskers and melting eyes. "Oh, all right. Half. You can have half mine."

Sofie licked her cheek lovingly. "You are a good girl, Lottie *ma belle*," she murmured, her bristly nose whiffling against Lottie's ear and making her laugh.

They ate the cakes, sitting rather uncomfortably

round the kitchen table and trying to feel like a family. No one mentioned what was going to happen now that Lottie's dad was back. How it was going to change things. No one seemed to want to.

Actually, Lottie did, very much, but she had no idea how to start the subject off.

Uncle Jack gratefully seized on Horace and his transformation instead. He had put a saucer of sunflower seeds on the table, and Horace was standing next to it, looking at them in a considering sort of way.

"They're good fat ones," Uncle Jack said encouragingly.

Horace picked one up in his beak, then dropped it again.

"Fancy a nice juicy mouse instead?" Danny asked cheekily.

Horace turned round and ignored him, but when Danny started making *too-whit*, *too-whoo* noises, he glared at him over his shoulder. "Children should be seen and not heard. Especially when they can't say anything more intelligent than that."

Danny just licked the chocolate off his fingers and smirked, but Uncle Jack sighed. "He does have a point. Um. Are you planning on doing that again, Horace? We might need to come to some sort of an arrangement. About your – um – feeding habits."

"Dad means, please don't eat the stock," Danny put in, and Lottie choked on a cake crumb.

"It was merely a moment of forgetfulness. A small error," Horace muttered grumpily. "I foolishly allowed the boy to irritate me. After the shock of Tom's return. . ."

Lottie nodded. Her father's arrival had thrown everyone off balance. It was odder still to hear Horace call him Tom. But the phoenix had known her father before he *was* her father, she supposed.

"You really haven't changed, all this time?" Tom was frowning. "How long is it?" he asked, his voice suddenly dropping. "How long have I been gone?"

"Eight years," Lottie whispered.

Tom went greyish pale under his tan, and mouthed it back at her. "Eight? I can't have been." He stared at the table, and then sighed. "Who am I kidding? Of course I can. But it doesn't seem that long. How can it be, when I don't remember?" he begged them.

27

"What do you remember?" Lottie asked him shyly.

Her father shook his head. "Almost nothing. The long journey back, that's all. Travelling. Stowing away on ships and lorries. Knowing that I had to reach somewhere important, but not knowing what the somewhere was. My home." He paused for a minute, and then added, "And the unicorns. I remember the unicorns." He dropped it into the conversation almost casually, then glanced at them all, as though he thought they might not believe him, and went back to staring grimly at the table.

Then he looked up, as everyone in the room seemed to draw in a sharp breath. "What?"

Uncle Jack put his coffee cup down slowly. "When you left, eight years ago, it was to go on an expedition to find unicorns. In the rainforests in the foothills of the Himalayas."

Tom nodded thoughtfully. "I found them. . ." he muttered. Then he shook his head. "But why don't I remember why I went? Or anything before?" He looked bewildered, and suddenly ill.

"I was doubtful about the unicorns. I didn't believe you. In fact, I told you it was a stupid, pointless, irresponsible thing to do," Uncle Jack told him. "No one really wanted you to go, but you were so sure that the rumours were true. You're sure they're real?" he asked, his voice shaking slightly, as though he'd always dreamed of this, and never dared hope it would happen.

But Lottie didn't care about the unicorns – not right this minute, anyway. "It was a set-up!" she burst out. "It was Pandora. It was her revenge, sending you away from Mum, and from me!"

Her dad gaped at her. "Who is Pandora? And your mother. . ." He groaned softly. "I didn't even think. Of course. Oh, this is so cruel, I don't remember her either. Where is she?"

"France," Lottie explained wearily. "For work. That's why I'm living here. We moved away after you disappeared. Mum doesn't understand about the magic, you see. Don't you know any of this?" she burst out crossly.

"No. Look, I'm sorry, Lottie. But I just don't. Tell me. Who's Pandora?"

Lottie looked helplessly at Uncle Jack. She really didn't want to tell her dad all about his mad enchantress ex-girlfriend; it was much too weird. But the thoughts racing and tumbling through her mind were too strong to hold back. She couldn't tell him, but she couldn't stop herself showing him.

Sofie snuggled lovingly into Lottie's lap, and lent her strength to the strange vision that suddenly appeared, floating over the table.

Everyone stared, silent and spooked as the glittering mists formed into a picture of a beautiful woman – beautiful, but frightening. She stood there laughing in a red dress, a curtain of long, white-blonde hair flying about her, and a young girl cowering in front of her.

Lottie heard her father's gasp of angry breath.

"That's Pandora," Lottie whispered. "And that's me. . ."

Then the image changed. Pandora's smile faded, and she seemed to look around, as though something had worried her. There was a strange sound, a drumming that gradually settled into hoofbeats, and an enormous creature appeared on the rocks above Lottie and Pandora. A unicorn.

Lottie had seen this before, of course, and Sofie had been there with her, but the others hadn't, even though she'd tried to explain to Uncle Jack and Danny what had happened. Fred had climbed out of her father's pocket and was standing on his trouser leg, twisting his tail in excitement, bouncing up and down and squeaking encouragement to Lottie and the unicorn, as the enormous silver-white creature chased Pandora away. *Frightened* her away, leaving Lottie and Sofie alone and shivering on Netherbridge Hill.

"Lottie," Uncle Jack murmured, as the image faded. "Oh, Lottie, I'm sorry. It's not that I didn't believe you, but I never thought it was like that. . ."

"Sshhh!" Sofie told him bossily. "There is more. Look!"

Lottie blinked. The glittering mist was swirling in front of them again, but she wasn't controlling it. She looked over at her father, and wondered if that was how she looked when she made visions happen, that slight frown, the faraway look in his eyes.

The silver-white unicorn was there again, but he was a different creature now. Still beautiful, but terribly sad. His head was hanging as he stared into a shallow, fast-running river – Lottie couldn't see into the water, but she guessed he was looking at his reflection.

Suddenly the silver unicorn threw up its head and uttered a loud cry, a strange triumphant noise. It wheeled around from the riverbank and galloped off through the trees, so recklessly that Lottie held her breath, sure that it would injure itself. The unicorn raced on and on, until the dark trees opened up into a misty clearing, where it slowed its headlong gallop till it stood still at last, its sides heaving, the long, sharp horn sparkling in a sudden burst of sunlight that lit up the long grass.

Then out of the sunshine came another unicorn, much smaller, and a rich, soft golden colour this time. She rubbed her head against the silver unicorn, and then they disappeared, fading away as they walked together into the sun.

"Do you remember that, then?" Lottie begged her father. "You made it do that. I didn't, did I? I definitely don't remember that part."

"That was my dream. . ." her father muttered. "I remember it now – everything's so vague and misty, but I remember the little golden unicorn. She reminded me of who I was – or at least, that I was *someone*. And it was you, of course. . ." He was frowning, staring at Lottie. "I hadn't understood. I was a trapped unicorn, and that golden creature came to lead me home. It was you, Lottie, all the time. You brought me home to you." He flung back his chair and hugged her, just the way she'd wished he would, whirling her round. "You clever, clever girl."

"I don't get it," Danny said, still staring at the air above the table, where now only a few dust motes glittered in the light from the kitchen window. "I thought you said Pandora made up the unicorns to make your dad go on that mad trip, Lottie?"

"No. No, they were real, I'm sure of it. I found them. You saw, didn't you?" Lottie's dad looked round at them all. "Couldn't you tell they were real?" He hugged Lottie tightly one last time, and gently set her down. "Maybe not, I suppose. But the unicorns are about the only thing I'm sure of. They were there, and so was I." He frowned. "So that was Pandora then? The woman in the red dress?"

"You don't remember her either?" Lottie asked gratefully. It would have been too much if he'd forgotten her mother but remembered Pandora, the spiteful, scheming witch who'd tried to turn Lottie into her own little slave.

Her father shuddered. "I think I'm quite glad I can't."

"She's really evil, Tom," Uncle Jack said gravely. "She's still around, too. She knows Lottie's your daughter, and she can't bear it. She loved you first,

33

you see. She didn't want you to belong to anyone else. She pounced on that rumour of unicorns eight years ago and wafted it in front of you, to send you away. She knew you'd always been mad on them."

"It wasn't just a rumour," Lottie's father said stubbornly. "I found them. I can feel them. But something made me forget everything that came before. Lottie, you think it was because of this Pandora?" Lottie's father asked her anxiously. "You need to stay away from her. She's dangerous."

Lottie glared at him. He had walked out and left her eight years ago – he couldn't just turn up and an hour later start acting all bossy and protective.

Her father's face fell. "Oh. Yes. I suppose – if your mother doesn't understand magic – you've had to deal with it all yourself. You don't need me butting in now."

Lottie gave him a half-smile. She felt as though she was balancing on a tightrope, trying to walk a dangerous path between her feelings and his. "Pandora knows who I am now. But actually, she didn't like me from the very first time she met me. I wouldn't let her in my mind, and that made her really cross. She's a control freak."

"You had really bad taste, Uncle Tom," Danny pointed out, carefully nibbling all the chocolate off his mini roll.

Lottie's dad frowned, but he looked bewildered, not angry. "I must have done," he agreed.

"She said she'd killed you," Lottie whispered. "It's why she was so angry to find I was your daughter. She thought she'd wiped you off the face of the earth, and then she found you'd left your blood and your magic behind after all."

"A legacy," her father murmured, gazing at her proudly. "Except I'm not dead. I wonder how she thought I was. If she was that strongly linked to me, you'd think she would have been able to tell."

"She didn't know the unicorn was you, the first time you came," Lottie said thoughtfully. "That was what I showed you before, when you chased her away on the hillside. But when you rescued me from her again, then she saw you properly, and she screamed. That's when I knew it was you, too. The first time you rescued me I thought it was Uncle Jack."

Her father was shaking his head wearily. "I rescued you. It seemed like dreams; I wasn't sure if it was real. The girl, and the dog, and that awful creature in the red dress. . ."

Lottie nodded. "It definitely happened. You were a great big silver unicorn, and you chased Pandora away. You said you'd always be there if I called for you." *It was the most like a father you've ever been,* she added to herself.

"I knew I had to make a journey," her father muttered. "There was something important. I knew that. And somehow I knew which way I had to go, which ships to stow away on." He smiled at their shocked faces. "I've magic enough to hide myself away when I need to, after all. I was coming back to you, my girl." His face was grim, but he laid his hand on Lottie's so gently. "I know I left you. But truly, I never meant to be gone for so long. And now I'm back, and I won't leave you again, Lottie, I promise. I won't just be a pretty horse in a dream; I'll protect you properly." Then he looked straight into her eyes. "I won't go, Lottie, unless you ask me to. You aren't sure about me. I'm not what you wanted, I can see that. I left you, I forgot you, and now I'm only half here. If you want me to let you carry on as you were before, I would understand. It's up to you."

Lottie gaped at her father. She hadn't expected him to see into all her doubts and confused resentment. "I – I don't know," she stammered. "I don't know what to say to you. I wished for you to come back. I saw you in so many dreams." She took a deep, steadying breath. "And now you are back . . ." She looked down at Sofie, her dark eyes meeting the little dog's, sharing a look of doubtful hope. ". . . we want you to stay."

3

It was true, Lottie thought to herself, up in her little attic bedroom. She did want her father to stay. It was very odd, though, knowing that he was there, in the room below hers. She wondered if he couldn't get to sleep either.

She kept thinking of things, that was the problem. How was she going to tell Mum? Was Danny OK? Was he lying awake next door, wishing that his mum would suddenly turn out to be alive too? What was she going to say to Ruby, and everyone at school? How was she going to explain that she had a father again?

Sofie padded up beside her. She had been curled up at the end of the bed like a little furry toy, breathing slowly and deeply, while Lottie thought grumpily how nice it would be to be able to sleep like that.

"I was not really asleep, Lottie," she purred, snuggling up next to Lottie's ear. "I thought you needed time to think. But I have given you lots of time now, and you are still wriggling about so much that I could not sleep even if I wanted to. You will have to keep still while we are talking; it is most annoying when you fidget."

Lottie chuckled. Sofie's bossiness always cheered her up. It was rather nice to have someone telling her what to do, someone looking after her.

"So. Is he how you remember him?" Sofie murmured. She was speaking aloud, but she was so close to Lottie's ear that she only had to breathe the words. It was soothing.

"I'm not sure. I don't really remember him much at all," Lottie admitted. "I was so little. And Mum wouldn't talk about him, so I don't even have stories about us together to remember." She sighed.

Sofie nudged Lottie's cheek gently. "You could make new memories, Lottie, *ma belle*. It is silly to fuss over not having any old ones, when your father is here with you now."

Lottie nodded. "I suppose you're right, but I can't help wishing he remembered me." She hesitated. "It feels as though he can't really have loved me very much, if he doesn't even remember," she admitted haltingly.

Sofie was silent, breathing lovingly into Lottie's ear. Then, a little later, she said, "I do not think that is so, Lottie. He loved you very, very much. And I think you know that deep down. There are memories of him. It is just that you cannot see them."

Lottie giggled. "Have you been wandering around in my brain, Sofie?"

"It is very interesting," Sofie said primly. "You do not mind?"

"No," Lottie said sleepily. "Tell me what you can see."

Sofie snuggled down next to her, and breathed into her ear again. "No, I will show you. Close your eyes and watch."

Lottie felt like saying that that didn't make sense, but she was too sleepy to explain this to Sofie. Instead she did as she was told. It was always the best option with Sofie around, anyway.

The blackness behind her eyelids felt soft and warm, and Lottie dreamed.

"Lottie! Lottie! Sssshhhh! Come quietly and see." Her father was half-whispering, and he sounded so excited. A very young Lottie raced across the grass towards him, dashing through the buttercups. He was crouched on a little rise, leaning over to look at something below them.

Lottie flung herself into his outstretched arm, curling in against him, and obediently hushed as he put a finger to his lips. "Look," he murmured into her ear, and turned her so she too was looking out across the little patch of meadow grass in front of them.

"Ohhh. . ." Lottie whispered delightedly. The air was full of dancing butterflies, skimming and whirling over the long grass that was splashed with red poppies.

"Aren't they pretty, Lottie? I knew you'd like them. The sunshine brings them out, you see. And they like the poppies."

"I want them," Lottie said wistfully. "Let's dance with them, Daddy!"

Her father smiled. "I don't know if they'll stay, Lottie. Try it. I think if I danced with them they'd fly off in a panic, but maybe you're small enough to do it."

Lottie stared anxiously at the butterflies. She wanted to be *with* them, not watching them. All of a sudden, she broke out of her father's arm, and raced headlong down the little slope into the centre of the flickering rainbow cloud. Then she froze. Would they simply disappear? But the butterflies continued to flitter around her, swooping down to rest on the tall flowers, then diving away again. She had wanted to dance, but she couldn't move; she was too fascinated by the fairy-like creatures. A tiny blue butterfly shot past her nose, and then seemed to hover, as if it was looking back at her. It had the most amazing purple furry body, and lilac-blue wings. It flicked them at her as it shot away.

Lottie stretched out her arms very slowly, stretching out each finger, just in case any of them looked like good butterfly resting places. *Please. . .* she thought hopefully. She looked longingly over at her father, and saw that his hands were held out towards her – no, to the butterflies – and he was beckoning.

The first butterfly was a soft, rich brown. Lottie was too young to have thought much about what colours meant, but she vaguely imagined that brown was boring. But this was a chestnut colour, and it was splotched with great blue circles, like blue eyes staring out of its wings. It had frilly edges too, Lottie noticed, as she watched it lazily opening and closing its wings, perched on the edge of her sleeve.

It was followed by another and another, till they were scattered thickly all over her arms like living bracelets, quivering gently in the sunlight. Lottie shivered deliciously, enjoying the fizzing in her blood, the lovely secret feeling that rushed over her sometimes when she saw animals she loved. Daddy had it too – all the animals talked to him. . .

Lottie smiled in her half-sleep. *Why don't I remember this?* she asked Sofie.

You will now, Sofie told her, yawning hugely and showing acres of teeth. *Go to sleep.*

The baby Lottie lifted her arms gently, wanting to see a shower of butterflies, and her jewelled coating fluttered away, swirling round and round her, as she laughed delightedly at her watching father, seeing how proud he was.

The sweetness of the dream – or the memory, Lottie wasn't quite sure which – stayed with her the next morning. She felt as though she knew her father so much more, just from that one little glimpse. She wondered if Sofie could somehow show him the butterflies too. Lottie got up, humming to herself, and ran downstairs. She wasn't sure if her dad would be down yet. He'd stayed up late the previous night with Uncle Jack, talking and listening, as his brother tried to tell him everything that had happened in the last eight years, and a lot more besides, in the hope that something would break the lock on his memories.

Lottie looked at him hopefully as she came into the kitchen. She still did a double take as she saw him and Uncle Jack together – it really did look like one Uncle Jack making toast, and another Uncle Jack scolding Fred the mouse and his friend Peach for stealing the sugar.

"You'll rot your teeth," the real Uncle Jack was telling them crossly. "I can do many things, but mouse dentistry is not one of them. Once they're gone, they're gone!"

Fred looked thoughtfully at the sugar bowl, and then at Peach. "Worth it?" he asked.

"Definitely." Peach nodded. He was a slightly darker pink than Fred, with a reddish line running down his back like the blush on a peach skin. He couldn't be called anything else.

Together they had levered out the largest lump of the smart French brown coffee sugar that Uncle Jack occasionally gave in and bought for Sofie, and were now lugging it between them over the table top. Lottie ducked under the table to see what they would do when they reached the far side, and laughed out loud to see a small pulley system involving a loose thread from the oilcloth and a bottle top. Fred would do anything for sugar, even inventing.

"That is *my* sugar!" Sofie stopped, appalled, in the doorway, as Fred and Peach trotted past, the sugar clasped lovingly in their arms. "Those mice are stealing *my* sugar!"

"They do love it too," Lottie told her apologetically. "Shall I put some in your coffee?" she suggested, trying to distract her.

Sofie gave her a stern look. "Do you think that I can be distracted from everything by food?" she asked Lottie pointedly.

"Most things?" Lottie suggested, in a hopeful voice.

Sofie watched her for a few seconds more, as though unsure whether it was too early in the morning to bother having a small tantrum. "Perhaps," she conceded graciously. "Yes, you may pour me some black coffee. With two lumps of *my* sugar. If those little *vermine* have left me any."

Lottie's father watched her fussing lovingly over the dog, a smile lurking in the lines around his eyes. Horace was perched on his shoulder, but he looked disapproving, as usual.

"Lottie, how much of your magic do you understand?" her father asked her suddenly, and Lottie looked up at him in surprise. He shook his head wearily. "Sorry, I seem to have forgotten tact as well as everything else. But you and Sofie – you seem so close. I just wondered. . ."

"Sofie is Lottie's familiar," Uncle Jack told him. "Between the pair of them, they're very strong. A friend of mine is teaching them, Ariadne. You knew her before you went, too," he added apologetically. Lottie wondered if he'd spent most of yesterday evening saying similar things.

Tom blinked, then closed his eyes altogether, and whispered, "Shadow?"

"Yes!" Lottie exclaimed delightedly. "Shadow is Ariadne's familiar."

Tom nodded, his eyes still closed. "A grey-striped tabby," he said slowly, but his voice was becoming more confident. "Bossy. A brilliant mouser. Sorry," he added, as someone gave an outraged squeak from the direction of the kitchen door. "And he loves climbing trees, doesn't he?"

There was a silence, as Lottie and Uncle Jack looked at each other helplessly.

Tom opened his eyes again, frowning at them. "I'm wrong, aren't I?" he decided dismally. "Shadow's not a cat."

"Oh, no, he is!" Lottie said eagerly. "It's just that. . ."

"You're remembering Shadow, all right," Uncle Jack said gently. "But he doesn't climb trees now, Tom. He's blind. It's been a while since you saw him, after all."

Lottie's father nodded, rather hopelessly. "Yes. Yes, of course." He tried to smile. "Ariadne, hmm? Even if my memories are out of date, judging by her familiar, she's very special. You're lucky to have her teaching you, Lottie."

He was trying so hard to be positive, it made Lottie want to cry. It also made her even more determined. She was going to get his memories back for him. He might have missed eight years of her life, but he wasn't going to lose everything else too.

A little of Lottie's hopeful mood had worn away by the time she left to meet her friend Ruby. They usually walked to school together, meeting at the bridge that was halfway between the shop and Ruby's house by the side of the river. Ruby knew most of the secrets about the shop. She could hear animals talk – some people couldn't, if they just didn't have the right sort of imagination. She had two gorgeous blue lizards of her own, who'd happily introduced themselves to Lottie the first time she went to Ruby's house. They claimed they were dragons, but Lottie wasn't sure whether or not to believe them. Seeing how much Ruby adored Sam and Joe, even before Ruby knew her pets could talk, had helped Lottie to trust her. She was so glad she had – it made a huge difference having someone to share all these weird new experiences with.

But what was she going to tell Ruby about her dad?

Lottie wasn't sure she was quite ready to break the news to anyone else yet. It was all still too strange and scary. Ruby knew about Lottie's encounters with Pandora, and the unicorn rescuing her. Pandora had put a spell on Ruby a few weeks before, in order to trap Lottie – she didn't care who she took down in her fight against the whole Grace family. Lottie had told her friend all about the strange unicorn who kept turning up in her dreams – but it was a big step from dreaming about her father to having him suddenly come home.

Actually, Lottie admitted to herself as she saw Ruby waving to her from the bridge, if her dad had remembered who she was, she wouldn't have had a problem at all. She just didn't want to tell anybody her own father didn't know her. Not even Ruby.

It was difficult to behave normally with such a huge secret hanging over her, though. Everything she tried to say seemed to come out wrong. Eventually, after Lottie had started and stopped about three different conversations, Ruby grabbed her by the arm and marched her over to a bench in an out-of-the-way corner of the playground.

"What's going on? You're talking rubbish and you keep going bright red. What aren't you telling me?"

Lottie stared at her, with her mouth open, and didn't say anything. Then she looked miserably at the ground.

"Are you not allowed to say?" Ruby asked sympathetically. She loved hearing about all the magical stuff that went on at the shop, but she understood that sometimes there might be stuff that had to be a secret even from her.

"It isn't that," Lottie muttered. "I will tell you. I just – I haven't got it all sorted out in my head yet.

I do want to tell you everything, Ruby, honestly. Please don't be mad at me."

Ruby hugged her. "Twit."

Lottie leaned against her friend for a moment and sighed, and felt a warm rush of love from Sofie. The dachshund sounded sleepy, and Lottie imagined that she'd been curled up snoozing on her velvet cushion in the shop, or perhaps on Lottie's bed. *You should tell her*, she yawned. *She would have good advice.*

Lottie blinked. She almost wanted to. But it was just so embarrassing. And what if someone overheard? She could just imagine what Zara Martin and her gang of mean little mates would make of it. It would go on for ever.

"OK. Tell me about your weekend then," Ruby said. "Your mum came over from France? Was it all right?"

Lottie smiled and shook her head. She'd almost forgotten in the drama about her dad. He'd arrived just after she had come back from seeing her mum off at the station. It was lucky he hadn't turned up a couple of hours earlier. Or was it? Maybe it would have been better for him to meet everyone at once? If he'd seen Lottie's mum, would it have brought his memory back?

Probably not. He would have forgotten her like he'd forgotten Lottie – even though her mum had been married to him for three years before he went. It would have been heartbreaking.

No, it was definitely better that she had missed him. At least now they had a chance to recover his memory before Lottie tried to bring her family back together. Because if she could help him heal, she might have a chance at having a mother *and* a father again. She needed him to help her explain magic to Mum. They had to try. Seeing her mum that weekend had made Lottie feel mean, almost cruel even, for not sharing the magical part of her life.

"It was really weird," she told Ruby now. "She fell in love with Barney. She had a rabbit when she was my age, she said, and it was like she forgot all that stuff she'd ever said about pets being dirty, and just not being an animal person." She lowered her voice. "I started to think we could even tell her about the shop. She was so different."

"Seems a pity she had to go back when you were getting on really well." Ruby sighed.

Lottie nodded. "She thought so too. She dropped a bombshell at the station – she told me she was

51

coming back home. She said she was going to tell her company that she couldn't do the Paris job any more. She even said they might sack her but she didn't care, she'd get another job!"

"That's brilliant!" Ruby gasped.

"Is it? What if she wants to go back to our old flat? She only rented it out to someone. We could go back in a few weeks." Lottie swallowed miserably.

"Oh." Ruby stared at her with anxious eyes. "You don't think she'd want to stay here then?"

Lottie looked up at her, and frowned determinedly. "I don't care if she doesn't want to. Mum thinks she's been doing the best she can for me all this time, getting really well-paid jobs, so we can have lots of clothes and holidays and stuff. But that's what *she* thinks is best. Now she has to listen to me. I'm not going back. I'm not leaving Sofie and the shop and you and my magic. Because it would all go if I left Sofie, and I was back with other people who don't even think magic's real. I bet it would just slip away."

"Wow," Ruby muttered. "What do you think she'll say?"

Lottie shrugged. "I haven't worked out how to tell her yet. But she'll probably phone tonight. She was going to talk to her boss today, and tell him she had to come back. She wasn't sure how long they'd want her to stay there." She nibbled one of her nails. "I don't want to tell her about the magic on the phone. I need to be able to see her for that. But I've got to explain that I can't leave Netherbridge. Otherwise she might start getting rid of the people in our flat, or something like that."

The bell for registration rang then, and Lottie sighed. She didn't feel like learning anything right now. It felt like she had more important things to worry about than fractions, which was what Mrs Taylor was sure to want them to do.

School didn't manage to distract Lottie from everything that was going on at home. Except for morning break, when Zara Martin had a row with her sidekick Bethany, who had rather stupidly managed to enjoy her weekend more than Zara had. Obviously this was not allowed. For once, Zara let her very careful guard slip, and did something horrible in front of a teacher. Usually, all the staff thought Zara was a little angel, but though Miss Stafford looked extremely shocked, she couldn't deny that Zara had just thrown an orange at Bethany (and missed by miles, but that wasn't really the point).

Remembering Zara's face as Miss Stafford put her in detention cheered Lottie up no end. It made her think, too, that Mum wouldn't want her to change school again in the middle of the year, when she'd just got settled. That was a really good, sensible reason for not moving. One that Mum was more likely to agree with than Lottie needing to stay with her talking dog.

When she got home, her dad was sitting at the counter, talking earnestly with Horace, and scratching the parrot's grey neck. Horace was gazing blissfully into the distance. Lottie's dad looked up and smiled when he saw her, and Lottie's heart jumped the same way it did when Sofie bounded towards her and flung herself into Lottie's arms. She smiled back, remembering the butterflies.

"Was school OK?" her father asked, a little awkwardly, and Lottie nodded back.

"School would be much better if Lottie learned to spell," Horace muttered. "But then you can't spell either, so I suppose I shouldn't expect it."

Lottie grinned at her dad. "Did you remember anything more today?" she asked him hopefully.

"Not much. I seem to know where to find all the different foods, and the ingredients in Jack's workroom. It's as though my hands remember, even if my brain doesn't. It'll come," he told her, trying to sound encouraging, and Lottie felt guilty. She should be the one encouraging him. She ducked down behind the counter to see if Sofie was asleep on her cushion, and the little dog yawned and stretched, knowing what she wanted before she asked.

"Oh, very well, Lottie. But it is very rude to wake people up demanding things. He had better have chocolate." She wriggled into Lottie's arms, and then up on to the counter, till she was standing with her small russet front paws on Lottie's father's arm.

Horace clicked his beak irritably, and Sofie snapped at him. "Sssh! I am concentrating."

Lottie leaned against the counter, her chin in her hands, and closed her eyes. She could feel Sofie drawing on her memories again, and linking them to her father's.

There she was – a tiny little curly-haired child, running through the field of butterflies. Lottie flicked her eyes open for a second to look at her dad.

His eyes were wide open, shocked, but so happy at the same time. Lottie closed her own eyes again contentedly.

It was like watching a beloved film, the memory unrolling so clearly before her now, the little girl dressed in jewelled butterflies.

I wish I could show Isobel. . .

Lottie jumped upright. That wasn't her!

She stared at her father. He didn't seem to have noticed the stray thought in there that couldn't possibly be part of Lottie's memory. It had been him. Watching his daughter's magic working on the butterflies, and wishing he could let his unmagical wife into the secret.

Sofie looked round at her triumphantly. *You see. We will mend him*, she promised. *It may take us a long time, but we will.*

For once, Lottie did her homework as soon as she got upstairs. She needed something to do until her mum called, and she might not be in the mood for more fractions if the call didn't go well. She'd taken one of the cordless phones upstairs with her, and she eyed it worriedly every so often. What was Mum going to say?

She was in the middle of a really hard question

56

when the phone suddenly shrilled at her, so loudly that she jumped and knocked it on to the floor.

Sofie growled crossly from the bed, where she'd been dozing, and Lottie scrabbled about on the floor. "Shhh, Sofie, it'll be Mum. I won't be able to hear her with you doing that."

Sofie's eyes suddenly widened, and she uncurled herself sinuously from the bed, flowing down on to the floor and across to Lottie's desk. There she stared demandingly up at Lottie, until she scooped her up.

"Hey, Mum." Lottie tried to sound cheerful, but she'd rehearsed this conversation in her head so many times today, and it had never turned out well.

"Lottie! I've spoken to my manager, and I've handed in my notice. She was very nice about it – she said she'd felt they were asking a lot of me to stay on, when this job was only meant to be for a few weeks. And I can leave in two weeks, Lottie! Isn't that wonderful?"

"Mmm!" Lottie put on an enthusiastic voice, but even she could tell it sounded false.

"What's the matter, Lottie?" her mum asked, sounding a little hurt. "I thought you'd be pleased!"

"Oh, I am, Mum. I really am. It's just. . ."

"What?"

"Are we going back to the flat?" Lottie whispered, clutching Sofie against her tightly.

Her mum was nodding at the other end of the phone line, Lottie could tell. She did when she was on work calls, and she thought the other person had made a good point. "I'm not sure at the moment, because I know the lettings agency have got someone in there. But they're only on a month's notice. I'm sure your uncle would let me stay for a couple of weeks before we go back, wouldn't he?"

"I don't want to go back!" Lottie gasped out quickly. There was no easy way to say it.

There was a silence, filled only by the strange buzzing of the phone. It hurt Lottie's ears.

"But, Lottie – you knew it was only a short stay with Uncle Jack," her mum said at last. "Don't you want to go back home? Get all our things out of storage? See your friends?"

Lottie swallowed, to stop herself from starting to cry. She couldn't afford to get all upset, and have Mum just think she was a silly little girl.

"I know that was the plan, but then you stayed in Paris for longer than you said, Mum. I like it here. I like the school, and I've got Ruby, she's a brilliant friend." It was almost true. She didn't exactly like school, but she didn't hate it either. And Ruby was brilliant. "I love living at the shop, Mum, and I've got Sofie now." Sofie jabbed her cold nose into the back of Lottie's arm. *About time!* "She's mine, Mum. And we couldn't have her in the flat. You couldn't have Barney, either," she added. Mum had loved the rabbit so much. "It's no pets allowed."

More silence. "Lottie, I want you back with me," Mum said helplessly. "I do see what you mean, but – I need you with me."

"Then come here!" Lottie gabbled. "Come and live here! We don't have to live at the shop, I know that might be weird, but we could have a little house here, couldn't we, please?" Lottie felt a bubble of silly laughter rising up in her tummy. She felt like telling her mum that actually, living at the shop was no problem, she could just share a room with Dad. Maybe not.

"Oh, Lottie, I just don't think that would work – we have our own lives back at home. We can't just give everything up. And there's a good chance I might be able to have my old job back, Lottie. I wasn't going to tell you, because I didn't want to get your hopes up. Wouldn't that be perfect? It's not certain, but they're thinking about it. Everything can go back to the way it was before." Lottie could hear the pleasure and relief and hope in her mum's voice. It seemed odd that she could be so happy about something that was destroying Lottie's world.

She shook her head, even though her mum couldn't see her. "No. No, Mum. You don't understand. I can't leave here now." She could feel Sofie quivering next to her – the dachshund usually felt like a solid ball of warm fur, but now she was a mass of buzzing, nervous wires.

"Lottie, I understand how you feel," her mum began.

"No, you don't!" Lottie half-shouted at her. "If you understood how I feel you would stay here with me!"

Lottie could her mother starting to shut herself away, to think of Lottie as a little girl who couldn't see sense. "I won't go! I can't go! You have to understand," she said, slowing herself down and trying hard to sound sensible. "I just can't."

"Lottie, my job is back at home—"

"You don't know that. And why can't you get a job in Netherbridge?" Lottie gasped out. She was losing here, she could feel it.

"I thought you would be so pleased," her mother murmured, sounding bewildered. "This is *good* news."

"Not for me. . ." Lottie told her, half-crying now.

"We had such a wonderful weekend together!" Lottie's mum was almost crying too.

Tell her! Tell her! Sofie howled into Lottie's mind. *She will never understand if you don't tell her the truth! You will leave me behind, she will make you!*

I can't! She won't understand. Not now. She needs to be here, to see.

"Mum, I know we had a good time at the weekend – you were really enjoying being here. Can't you think about it? Please?" Lottie was trying hard to keep the wobble out of her voice, to sound sensible and calm, but it was so hard.

"Lottie, the shop isn't our home. We have a home, you and me together," her mum insisted.

"It's not home any more," Lottie burst out, before she knew what she was saying. There was a silence on the other end of the line, and Lottie closed her eyes miserably. "I'm sorry, I didn't mean it like that."

"Lottie, we'll talk about this another time," her mother's voice was carefully under control, as though really she wanted to yell, like Lottie did. "We both need to calm down. I'll call you again soon." There was a pause; then she added, very quietly, "I love you, Lottie."

It sounded as though she was staking a claim. Then there was a click, and then nothing.

4

"Lottie." Someone was tapping at her door. "Lottie?" Lottie rolled over and looked up, wearily. "Your uncle says it's dinner time. Lottie, what's wrong?" Her father, who had been hovering uncomfortably outside the door, as though he wasn't sure if he was allowed in, now strode over towards her and crouched by her bed.

Sofie licked his cheek affectionately, and Lottie tried to smile. "I'm all right," she muttered. She still felt torn between wanting to be angry with him for deserting her, and wanting to protect him. His lack of memory made him seem very fragile, even though he was so big.

Her father did that strangely familiar eyebrow raise again, and Lottie couldn't resist smiling this time.

"Was it a phone call?" her dad asked, noticing the phone left abandoned in the middle of the floor.

Lottie nodded, and sighed. Why not tell him? He didn't remember her mother, so it wouldn't really upset him, would it? Since they'd shared the memory of the butterflies, and she'd seen how much she'd loved him as a tiny child, it seemed to make it easier to talk to him now.

"It was Mum," she said quietly.

"Oh." Her dad rubbed a hand over his face, and looked worriedly at her. "Um. Is she OK?"

"Nope." Lottie rubbed Sofie's ears. "You know we told you she was working in France?"

Her father nodded, frowning as though he was trying to follow this carefully.

"She's coming back."

"But . . . don't you want her to?" The frown had deepened.

"Yes, of course I do! But she's not coming back here. She wants to go back to where we used to live. Our old flat. It's on the other side of the country, and I'd never see Uncle Jack or Danny or my friends. I couldn't take Sofie, Dad, don't you understand?" Lottie scowled at him. "Why are you smiling?"

Her father was definitely looking happy, a small, unconscious smile just lurking at the corner of his mouth. "You called me Dad. You haven't called me anything up till now."

Lottie's eyes widened, and she wriggled uncomfortably on the bed, feeling embarrassed. "Well – you are my dad. It just slipped out."

"I like it," he told her, smiling. "Very much."

"I wouldn't see you either," Lottie pointed out quietly. She looked up at him, flushing pink. "What are you going to do about her?"

Her dad uncurled himself from his crouching position on the floor, and sat down next to her. "Mustn't forget dinner," he muttered. "I don't know, Lottie. How can I see her? I abandoned you both, as far as I can tell, though everyone's tried to avoid telling me that. It might not have been on purpose, but I can't come back to her now, not when I don't remember who I am, let alone who she is. I'd be better off staying dead, I should think."

Lottie shivered, and he put an arm around her shoulders. "I'm sorry. Horrible thing to say. But do you see what I mean? Wouldn't it be almost worse to have me back the way I am now?" He squeezed her a little tighter. "Haven't you thought that?"

"No!" Lottie protested. Then she looked up at him sadly. "Maybe a little . . . but your memory's going to come back," she added, trying to sound confident. He *had* remembered Horace, and Shadow, and there had been that one little thread of thought. . . If she showed him more of her memories, surely it would help?

"Then you can meet Mum again, when you remember things." She stared at her fingers. "I want to tell her about the magic. I'm sure I can make her understand. You never told her, you see, and I think that's why she took me and left after you'd disappeared. She must have felt that people were hiding things from her. I felt like that here, before I knew, and that was only a couple of weeks. She lived here for years."

"I wonder why I kept it a secret," her dad murmured.

"She was very different from Pandora," Lottie said hesitantly. "Maybe you wanted to keep it that way. But your magic must have been such a special part of you. It is for me. I can't keep it from her. It just isn't fair. Especially if I'm telling her I won't leave here, I've got to explain why."

"You should have told her on the telephone," Sofie put in, flapping her ears vigorously.

"It wasn't the right time," Lottie disagreed. "She would just think I was being overimaginative. She's always saying that. I need to show her. I'm going to ask Barney if he'll help – Barney's a rabbit," she explained to her dad. "The sweet grey one in the cage opposite the counter?"

"Oh, yes. Nice, but not hugely bright?"

Sofie sniffed. "He is *un imbécile*," she muttered.

"But Mum thinks he's gorgeous. She had a rabbit when she was younger, which is really weird because she's always been totally against me having a pet at all. But if Barney talks to her, she might believe me, you see."

Her father nodded. "So you want to stay?"

"Of course I do!" Lottie looked up at him, in sudden fear. "You're going to stay, aren't you? You won't go again?"

Her father smiled. "No. I may have hardly any memories, but I trust my feelings. I belong here. I knew it when I first walked in. The smell was right. And the room I slept in last night seems familiar." He shivered. "But rather empty."

Lottie nodded. "We should go down. Uncle Jack gets grumpy when people don't come and eat his food. Did he add anything weird to the stew after I'd gone?"

Her dad looked slightly worried. "Quite a lot of very odd-looking mushrooms," he admitted.

Sofie jumped down from the bed. "Are you feeling lucky?" she asked mischievously.

Somehow, talking to both her parents had changed things for Lottie. She felt much closer to her dad. It was the first time she had really understood how he was feeling. And he seemed as confused by his behaviour eight years ago as she was.

Talking to her mum had made her realize how lucky she had been in Netherbridge – getting on well with her uncle and Danny, and finding Ruby. So much so that when she met her friend at the bridge on Tuesday morning, she gave her a hug.

Ruby looked mildly surprised. "What was that for?"

Lottie shrugged, and smiled at her sheepishly. "I don't know. Just wanted you to know – something. That I'm lucky to have you, I suppose. Can you come round after school? I've got something to show you."

"Oooh, is your uncle getting a new pet for the shop?" Ruby asked excitedly. "Did those bluebirds that could change colour come?"

Lottie shook her head. "No, he says that was a scam, they were painted, poor things, some sort of light-reflecting paint." She grinned. "Actually, he sent Henrietta in to the dealer who was selling them, and she opened their cage and let them all go." Henrietta was Uncle Jack's special homing mouse. He used her to discourage people he felt shouldn't be allowed to have animals. She had a fantastic way with chewing through electrical cables, and she put people off pets beautifully, and then came home to the shop. "No, it's something different. Will you come and see?" Lottie gulped. It felt like a big step.

Ruby nodded, picking up on the seriousness of this. "Course. Lottie, are you OK?"

"Mmm. I think so." Lottie smiled at her, noting Ruby's worried eyes, and knew she was doing the right thing.

Ruby nodded slowly, and they walked on, not talking. Just as they got to school, Ruby suddenly turned to Lottie, looking excited. "I remembered what I meant to ask you. It's your birthday at the end of November, isn't it? So it's this month! Do you know what you're going to do yet?"

Lottie blinked. "I'd forgotten," she said, her voice shocked. Imagine forgetting her own birthday! It just showed how mad things were at the moment. Normally she would have been making present lists and planning the party months in advance. "What do people normally do for birthdays round here?" The last few parties she'd been to, with people from her old school, had all been ice-skating parties. It had been the big thing that year.

Ruby shrugged. "Depends. I had a sleepover for my last party, and Zara broke my CD player. On purpose."

"You *invited* Zara?" Lottie asked, sounding amazed.

Ruby sighed and looked at her, rather shamefaced. "Not exactly. . . I invited the girls I liked from our class. Lucy. Keisha. Becca. You know, the ones who aren't Zara's gang. But they all said they couldn't come, and I was really upset." Ruby blinked hard. It obviously still hurt. "So I asked Lucy why she couldn't come – that was really embarrassing. I felt like I was being all whiny, you know, *Why don't you like me, Lucy?* And she told me that she really wanted to come, but Zara had found out I was having a party – she nicked Keisha's invite out of her bag – and she'd told them if they went to a party she wasn't invited

70

to, she'd make their lives hell. So they said they couldn't go."

Lottie felt like hitting something, just watching the expressions on Ruby's face as she told the story. "What did you do?"

Ruby stared at her feet. "I invited Zara. Not all the rest of them; I told Zara I wasn't allowed any more than four, and that was true, actually, Mum said over her dead body was I having any more. Anyway, she totally ruined it and I hated the whole thing. I should never have given in, I'd have had a better time just going out for a meal with Mum and Dad. But then they'd have gone into a panic about me not having any friends, and my mum's awful when she gets like that."

Lottie nodded sympathetically. "I don't think I'd get away with a sleepover, do you? Someone would be bound to go and get a drink of water and find Fred and Peach tap-dancing or something."

Ruby giggled. "Or Sofie would tell them they were stupid. No, you're right, too dangerous. Maybe you could go to the cinema in Sandford?"

Lottie slumped down on to a bench. "I don't know if I'll still be here by the end of the month," she admitted grimly.

"What?" Ruby squeaked, thumping down beside

71

her. "Why? What's going on? Did your mum call you last night?"

"Uh-huh. She's coming back, and she wants to go home. I had a massive row with her about it. It was awful. I feel really guilty, but at the same time I just can't let her take me away. Can I?" Lottie begged.

"No way." Ruby shook her head, so that her bunches of dark-red hair whirled. "You mustn't."

"And – well, you'll see later. . ." Lottie added. It was too tricky to explain a sudden father. Ruby would have to wait and see.

"Don't scream or anything," Lottie cautioned her friend as she pushed open the shop door.

Ruby stopped dead on the doorstep. "It's not something horrible, is it?" she asked suspiciously.

"No, but it's a bit surprising," Lottie sighed. "Come on."

Both her dad and Uncle Jack were sitting behind the counter, and Horace was sitting on her dad's shoulder. At least, she was fairly sure it was her dad. She had to do a mental check on which one of them was more tanned. They were reading a price list from one of Uncle Jack's suppliers, and enthusiastically circling things in red pen. Lottie smiled hopefully to herself at the sight. She hadn't thought of it before, but working in the shop was sure to help her father remember. He seemed to have more memories of animals than anything else, and he was much more relaxed with animals than people, so perhaps the memories would just slip back naturally? He'd already said he remembered where things were in the workroom and the feed store.

Tucking this away for more thinking later, Lottie pulled Ruby further into the shop. Her friend stood in front of the counter, looking from Jack to Tom and back again. Then she looked at Lottie with her mouth open.

"Dad, this is my best friend, Ruby," Lottie said firmly. "I've brought her home to meet you." Then she smiled. Her father had mostly looked confused and worried ever since he'd arrived, except for yesterday when she'd called him Dad for the first time. But when she introduced him to Ruby, he looked enormously pleased, and blushed bright red, like Danny did sometimes.

He leaned over the counter and shook Ruby's hand vigorously, then sat back looking shy. "It's so good to meet you," he said softly. "Er. Has Lottie explained?"

"No," Ruby told him, eyeing Lottie accusingly. "She just said she wanted me to see something. Have you been back long? You can't have been. . ."

"I arrived on Sunday," Lottie's father agreed. "But. . ." He gave her an embarrassed smile. "I seem to have lost my memory."

"Oh!" Ruby looked as though she didn't know what to say. "Um, all of it?"

"Practically everything," Lottie put in. "Even me."

"That must be really scary," Ruby said. It made Lottie remember again that that was the good thing about Ruby. She was much better at worrying about other people's feelings than Lottie was.

"It is," her dad agreed gratefully. "And I can't help feeling furious, and half the time it's with myself. It's not good. But I'm here, and I have Lottie and Jack and Danny. I didn't really know what I was doing until I got back here, it was all just a blur." He smiled. "Lottie has big plans for getting my memory back."

Ruby nodded. "She will," she told him, with the utmost confidence. "Lottie doesn't give up."

Lottie scuffed her foot on the floor, feeling shy. She'd just been thinking how good Ruby was at summing people up, but she hadn't expected her friend to do it to her.

She is right, Sofie told her lovingly. *You are most determined. Like me.*

"Oh, Lottie, I'm so pleased for you!" Ruby told her, up in Lottie's room. She was sitting on the bed stroking Sofie, her eyes shining.

"You liked him, then," Lottie asked shyly.

"Of course!" Ruby gave her a sharp look. "Imagine having a dad who can talk to animals, and who's been on amazing adventures. And he's just *nice*, as well. Were you worried I wouldn't like him?"

"He doesn't remember me," Lottie muttered. "I know it isn't his fault, but it's still weird. I – I think I love him, but he's just suddenly arrived, and he doesn't really feel completely like my dad yet. I wanted to know what you thought." But she felt a pleased little glow inside. She trusted Ruby.

Ruby leaned back against the wall, staring at the ceiling. "So how are you going to get his memory back?"

"I'm not sure," Lottie told her, frowning, and leaning back against the wall too. "Sofie showed me a memory I didn't know I had, from when I was tiny, and he was still here. Then I got her to show my dad too, and he definitely remembered another part of it; it was like he added a bit of his memory to mine. But he didn't realize he'd done it, and I didn't want to put him off, so I kept quiet about it. But maybe we could do that more." She looked hopefully at Sofie, who nodded at once – she loved being important. "And I was going to ask Ariadne to help too. But when I ask her that sort of thing she always says I have to look deep inside myself to find the answer. Sometimes I think that means she just doesn't know," Lottie added suspiciously.

"He is *your* father, Lottie," Sofie sighed, rolling over and letting Ruby stroke her stomach, which she very rarely allowed. "Up. Up. Left a little. Ah. . ."

"Why did he come back now?" Ruby asked suddenly.

"What do you mean?"

"Why now, not before? Something must have changed," Ruby explained.

"Well. . ." Lottie worked through the snippets her father had told them. "He's sure he found the unicorns. And he had dreams like I had, where he *was* a unicorn, and so was I. He says he followed me."

76

Ruby frowned. "Like the time you went galloping with him? He knew who you were then, didn't he? Didn't he say he was coming back to you?"

Sofie suddenly twisted over and sat up, panting eagerly. "She's right, Lottie." She ducked her head down and then shook her ears briskly, as though she was shaking something away. "You told me about it." Sofie had been very jealous of Barney the rabbit, and hadn't been part of the dream where Lottie was a unicorn too. She still found it difficult to talk about. "He told you he was trying to come back to you. Do you see what that means?"

Lottie shook her head doubtfully.

"It is like your father said yesterday! He was in some strange world where he'd forgotten everything, until you called him. You were the one who called him back." Sofie stared at Lottie, her black eyes sparkling with delight.

Lottie and Ruby only stared back at her, and she sighed in exasperation.

"I really didn't call him, Sofie!" Lottie said, frowning. "How could I? I thought he was dead! The unicorn just turned up – I didn't have anything to do with it."

"*Imbécile!*" Sofie yapped. "Of course you did! He

has been away for years and years, Lottie, with no way to return, because he did not know what to come back to. Then all of a sudden he knows he must make a journey. That is not chance! What has happened in the last few weeks, huh?"

"Lottie, she's right!" Ruby exclaimed, sitting up suddenly.

"Why does everybody else understand this and not me?" Lottie complained.

Sofie rolled her eyes. "You found your magic, Lottie! When you and I joined together! That is how he was able to return – because you found your power and it called to him! Your magic is his magic; you are bonded to him like you are to me."

"That sounds about right," Ruby agreed. "His journey back from the rainforests must have taken ages, even if he set off just when you discovered your magic and started using it."

Lottie smiled. She had been the one to call her father back from his exile! She loved the idea. "It doesn't help, though," she sighed. "I called him here, but I didn't bring his memory back with him."

"Of course it helps!" Sofie snapped. "If you can summon him out of a deep spell – which is what it sounds like – then you can pull his memory back too." But she didn't sound too sure, Lottie noticed.

"It's not as if I did it on purpose," Lottie sighed. "Could you get into his mind, the way you did with me and the dream about the butterflies last night?" she asked Sofie slowly.

"No. I can only do that because I am your familiar. I do not think it would work with anyone else."

"Oh." Lottie sighed. "Then we'll have to rely on using my memories to remind him. It might work, though it's bound to be a bit hit and miss."

Sofie nodded. "A very good idea. You see? I told you it would all be *parfait*." And she beamed round at them both smugly.

5

Lottie was planning another memory session with Sofie the next afternoon, and she raced home from school to round up Sofie and her dad. She wanted to get started as soon as she could.

But as soon as she put her hand on the shop door, she knew something was wrong. Her dad was standing there, in the middle of the shop – the strangely quiet shop, which was humming with fear. Lottie shut the door behind her, and the bell clanged ominously. But her father and the woman in the red dress hardly seemed to hear it.

"Oh!" Lottie gasped, without meaning to, and immediately wished she could hide. She had known that Pandora would come back some time, but she hadn't been ready for it yet.

I should have known, she thought to herself. *Dad*

could feel her chasing him when he was travelling back. He gave his secret away, protecting me. As soon as she knew he was still alive, she must have started trying to find him by magic. I should have been ready, but I'm not; I've had enough to think about with trying to have a dad again!

Sofie crept towards her, her belly low to the ground. *I am glad you are back,* she whispered silently.

How long has she been here? Lottie asked.

Only about five minutes. Danny is not back from school, and your uncle has gone to see Ariadne. Your father told him to go, he said he could look after the shop. But then she came.

Pandora and Lottie's father still seemed not to have noticed that Lottie was there. It was as though they were locked together in a world of their own, slowly circling round each other in the centre of the room.

Gradually, the creatures in the cages round the walls were creeping out again from their hiding places under their bedding. A few of the more daring mice, like Fred and Peach, even went so far as to climb out and sit on the shelves, their tails dangling, and watch as though this were some strange sort of entertainment. Giles the hamster was stomping up and down the counter, growling in a warlike fashion. But Pandora ignored him.

"I'm really amazed that you dared to come back," she said coldly. "I would have thought you'd have the sense to stay away."

Lottie's father looked at her politely, raising his eyebrows. "Yes?" he murmured. "Aren't you rather more amazed that I was *able* to come back? After all, I have been reliably informed that I was supposed to die out there."

Pandora simply smiled. "You shouldn't listen to gossip. And I don't think your sources are reliable at all. An overemotional little girl?"

Lottie fought back a desire to join the argument. She wanted to kick Pandora, but that would just fit the little-girl description.

"So you didn't have anything to do with sending me away, then?" Tom asked her.

Pandora looked down, her long white-blonde hair falling charmingly across her face. "I was upset," she explained, a wheedling tone coming into her voice. At least, that was how Lottie heard it. She had a horrible feeling that to her father it was meant to sound soft and loving. "You betrayed me – I always loved you, and the deepest love is only moments away from hate."

Lottie's father laughed. "I have a strong feeling you could argue your way out of anything, if only the person listening cared." He leaned forward. "But I don't. Don't bother sweet-talking me. I didn't recognize my daughter, I won't know my own wife, and *I don't know who you are*."

Pandora stared back at him, her eyes round with surprise, but still jewel-hard and calculating.

"You don't remember me?" she asked him sharply.

"I have no memory beyond the last few weeks."

Pandora wound a hand into her hair, hard enough that Lottie thought it must be hurting. She stood watching him silently, only her eyes flickering as the thoughts raced through her mind. "What happened then, to bring you back – oh! The girl. Her awakening power, I suppose." Pandora turned then, and swept a glance over Lottie, shivering by the door. "I wouldn't rely on her. I could heal you, you know. Bring all your memories back." She stepped towards him, one hand stretched out, and Lottie flung herself forward. But her father put up his own arm and swept Pandora away.

"I believe what my family have told me," he said, his voice like ice. "I don't want my mind recovered through you. My memories picked over, discarded when they didn't fit your version of events. I may be blank, but I'm not that stupid."

Pandora stepped back, frozen-faced, as though for a moment she really had expected him to let her touch him, and hold him, and break into his head. Like she had done so many times before, Lottie realized, shaking.

The enchantress smiled sweetly at Lottie, and swept her gaze along the row of cages, so that the mice dived back in and hid themselves again. Then she stalked out, passing Lottie, and stroking a gentle hand across her hair.

Lottie shuddered, as though a spider had just walked across her face, and Pandora's expression hardened. She looked ugly, and she slammed the door hard enough to crack the glass.

Lottie's dad strode over towards her. "Lottie, did she hurt you? She touched you, didn't she?"

Lottie leaned against him, still shaking, and Sofie pressed against Lottie's legs, her ears and tail drooping. "She thought Lottie might be distracted watching her argue with you. She tried to attack her mind again."

"Lottie! Lottie! Are you all right?" Lottie's dad grabbed her arms and shook her.

"I'm fine, stop shaking me. She didn't do anything. Ow, Dad, stop it, honestly!"

"Good." He hugged her tightly. "I'm sorry, you weren't saying anything, and I didn't know. . . I was scared that. . ."

"She has tried before," Sofie said flatly. "She caught us once, but you came, and you sent the fire in Lottie's mind away."

Lottie's dad hustled them into the kitchen and pushed Lottie into a chair. Then he sat down himself on the edge of the table, pressing his hands into his eyes. "*Why* can't I remember any of this?" he groaned. "I don't see how she can be stealing those memories too. Unless . . . I suppose I don't remember things fully when I was with the unicorns. Maybe that's it."

"She won't stop," Lottie told him, in a small voice.

Her dad tried to smile, but it looked strained. "Try not to worry, Lottie. In a way, I think she's made it harder for herself. Because I can't remember when I knew her before, she can't use it to trap me. There's nothing for her to catch on to." He leaned down to hug her. "What was it you were planning with Sofie at breakfast this morning?" he asked brightly. "I saw the two of you eyeing me."

He reminded her of Mum suddenly, being a cheerful parent, trying not to let her see that he was worried.

Lottie blinked. It seemed a very long time ago. "Oh – yes. We thought we could try showing you my memories again. To see if it helped?"

Her dad nodded. "It's a good idea. Maybe not right now, though?" He was frowning with weariness, and Lottie smiled, biting back what she really wanted to say. She could hardly tell him that it wasn't fair; she wanted him to get his memory back *now*. She needed him. And she had a horrible feeling that he might need every power and magic and memory he'd ever had, for when Pandora came back.

Lottie couldn't stop brooding about ways to drag her father's memories back. Ruby kept having to nudge her at school the next morning, when their teacher was starting to look suspicious. At lunch time she pulled Lottie over into a quiet corner and told her to snap out of it. "I can't keep Mrs Taylor off your back all afternoon too, Lottie! What's the matter?"

Lottie tried to smile, and managed an apologetic grin. "Just the same stuff. I promise I'll concentrate this afternoon."

She managed it, but as soon as Ruby had left her halfway home, Lottie was back to tussling with the memory problem, which was why she didn't even notice Pandora lurking in the doorway of her own strange little shop, ready to seize Lottie's arm. She drew her inside before Lottie could gather herself together enough even to squeak, and pushed her back against the counter.

"*Help!*" Lottie screamed and Sofie immediately woke up with a frenzy of barks.

"Ssshh!" Pandora snapped at her. "I'm not going to hurt you, you stupid girl. I just want to talk to you."

She was interrupted by a furred black and ginger bullet which suddenly appeared, shooting into Lottie's arms.

"Sofie! You went through a door!" Lottie gasped.

"Two," Sofie corrected her. "I came through the one at home too. You did not know I could do that, did you?" she added smugly. Then she eyed Pandora. "What does she want?"

Pandora eyed Sofie frostily. She clearly did not appreciate negotiating with a dog. Her own dogs, two beautiful Salukis, were pressed tightly against her legs, flanking her like bodyguards. "I have a proposition for you," she suggested, trying to smile and merely showing her teeth.

Lottie and Sofie watched her guardedly, and said nothing.

"I could see that your father's loss of memory is distressing, Lottie—"

"You caused it," Lottie told her, in a flat tone.

Pandora shrugged. "Hardly. I merely put him in the way of certain people."

Don't, Sofie whispered in Lottie's head. *She wants you to get angry. Remember what happened last time?*

Lottie nodded fractionally. She could never forget the feeling of being held a prisoner in her own head. She wondered miserably for a moment if that was what it felt like for her father, clawing at walls in his memory. She stared coldly at Pandora, determined not to allow herself to be trapped.

Pandora smiled silkily, and Lottie could feel soft green tendrils floating around her mind, as the enchantress automatically tried every way she knew to win Lottie over. She smiled to herself and repeated a spell that Ariadne had taught her a few days before, which withered the green shoots black and stung Pandora sharply. If being angry worked against Lottie, surely anger would throw Pandora off-balance too? She had practised this with

Ariadne and her new cat familiar – the gorgeous, slim, silky-furred Tabitha. Tabitha was training to take over from Shadow and was amazingly strong when working with Ariadne, but she had lost her concentration and fallen over backwards under the kitchen table when Lottie and Sofie hit her with this spell. She had stayed on her back with her legs in the air for half an hour, and Ariadne had been worried enough to call Uncle Jack for advice. Lottie had felt quite guilty.

She felt no guilt whatsoever about unleashing it on Pandora. Unfortunately it did not have the same dramatic effect. She merely shook her fingers, as though Lottie had stung her physically, and her eyes grew darker, her brows drawing together in a calculating look. It was horrible. She was sizing Lottie up, but it wasn't just that. She looked as though she had just seen something rather delicious, and she wanted it. Now.

She wants you, Sofie muttered, wriggling uncomfortably. *Us. I wish she would not stare at us as if we were dinner. I am not gateau. She looks at me like I look at gateau. With very good coffee.*

"I have been thinking, dear Lottie, that it's such a pity we don't get on. I really think we could be such very good friends, if only we could start again." Her eyes were growing hungrier, if anything.

Lottie tensed, waiting for another attack, but none came. Instead Pandora smiled, a greedy, excited smile, and stretched out a hand to Lottie. Sofie shrank back against Lottie's chest, hissing quietly.

"I have an offer, Lottie. One that I think you should consider very carefully." She paused. "I would like to take over your education."

Lottie was so surprised she laughed out loud. Was Pandora mad?

Pandora's smile faded for a moment, but then it was back, determinedly. "You may think I'm joking, Lottie. But I'm quite serious. Think about what I can give you."

"I don't want to learn magic your way," Lottie snapped back. "I don't want to be like you!"

"You might feel differently, if you had any idea what I can do. . ." Pandora smiled. "But that isn't all that's at stake, Lottie."

Lottie frowned. Pandora looked so confident, as though she didn't think Lottie could possibly resist her. What was she planning?

"As you said before, I am – unfortunately – responsible for your father's . . . shall we say, *misfortune*? Because that suggests that with good fortune, a little luck, it could all be put right." The dark eyes were fixed on Lottie's now, and Lottie's fingers tensed on Sofie's neck.

"A little luck. Or a little daughter-love, Lottie. That's all it would take, you know."

Lottie stared at her. "You mean, you could get it back? You could get *him* back?"

Pandora's smile was horribly triumphant now, but Lottie hardly noticed. "All of him, Lottie darling."

"The way he was before?" Lottie whispered.

"Exactly," Pandora nodded.

"If I become your apprentice?"

"You wouldn't regret it, Lottie. I really am a great deal more powerful than Ariadne. And rather more experienced."

Do not say yes now. . . Sofie murmured. *Tell her you have to think. Lottie, please!*

Lottie shook her head, as though clearing a mist from behind her eyes. *She had us,* she told Sofie. *Only a little, but she was there. Wow. She really is good.*

So are we. Do not sell yourself too lightly, Lottie.

Lottie nodded. "I need to think," she told Pandora.

Pandora shook back her long white-blonde hair, and the scent of it filled the room, thick and chokingly sweet. "I can't wait long," she said, still smiling.

"I know. I'll come back and tell you soon. I need to think." Lottie backed slowly away towards the door, unsure if Pandora would let her go so easily. The strange little ornaments in Pandora's shop sparkled and leered at her, whispering and laughing to each other. They were all parts of Pandora's magic, Lottie thought to herself, her mind working away without her meaning it to. Little spell-spies that she sent out, far and away. They knew Lottie would be back.

"Just bear in mind, Lottie, that your father is not the only person you care about."

She said it very quietly, just as Lottie laid her hand upon the door, and the words seemed to float in the air as Lottie dragged her heavy, half-reluctant footsteps away down the road.

6

"I can't go home," Lottie muttered, standing in the street, clutching Sofie close, and looking up and down the road like a hunted creature. "Not yet. I can't see Dad just yet. Where can we go?"

"Ariadne," Sofie yapped. "We need to talk to her. We should see what she thinks."

Lottie nodded slowly. She felt exhausted. "Yes, all right. Come on then." She walked quickly to Ariadne's flat, a few streets away, and she was halfway up the stairs before she suddenly stopped. "Maybe we shouldn't talk to Ariadne about it?" Lottie wondered. "I mean, she's bound to say no, isn't she? She wouldn't want me to go and be someone else's apprentice."

"You are that good an apprentice?" Sofie asked slyly, nudging a cold nose up against Lottie's neck.

Lottie flushed slightly. "I didn't mean it like that. Oh, I don't know what I meant." She sat down on the steps and laughed quietly. "This is where we came after we sneaked into Pandora's house, isn't it? When we found the photograph." The photograph that had told Lottie about her father and Pandora, giving her the clue that unravelled their whole story. "What are we going to do, Sofie?" she asked softly. "I don't even know whether to believe her or not."

"Oh, she meant it," Sofie told her grimly. "I am ready to swear."

"Then how can we say no?" Lottie's voice was a desperate moan. She didn't want to be Pandora's apprentice. She was happy learning from Ariadne, knowing that one day she would have powers like her teacher's. She didn't want to be the same as Ariadne, but that wasn't what was going to happen. Ariadne was teaching her to be herself – just better. Pandora would make her another Pandora.

"Or she will use you all up, and throw you away like a piece of rubbish," Sofie muttered, listening in to Lottie's thoughts.

Lottie nodded miserably. "But she might bring his memory back. She could, I'm sure she could.

What sort of daughter would I be if I didn't give him the chance to remember who he is?"

"What sort of father has he been to you?" Sofie's eyes were dark and velvety with love.

"That isn't the point," Lottie sighed, remembering the butterflies. "He would have been wonderful; it was Pandora who sent him away."

"He went in the first place."

Lottie glared at her. "Sofie, you *like* him! You told me I should be nicer to him!"

"But I *love* you. And if you go to Pandora, I will have to come with you. And I do not want to be her creature." Sofie shook her ears, shaking the idea away.

Lottie gazed at her, horrified at the thought.

"And not just because of those mad, skinny dogs," Sofie added. She hated the fact that Pandora's Salukis were so much larger than she was.

"She would have you too," Lottie muttered. She hadn't thought of it that way. Of course Sofie would come with her. That was what they had been fighting for, all this time, to stay together. It was why she wanted her perfect two-parent family back again, so that the important things wouldn't have to change. "She can't have you. I won't let her."

"Well, I am not going to leave you alone with that – that *harpie!*" Sofie snapped. "If you go, I go."

"I won't then," Lottie said miserably. But that meant condemning her father to live without his memories for ever.

"He can make new ones," Sofie said matter-of-factly. "And anyway, I thought we were going to find them for him? We do not need her. We found the butterflies, did we not?"

"Why are you two sitting on my stairs?" An amused voice floated down from above them, and Lottie looked up to see Ariadne peering over the banisters, her red hair trailing down towards them. "I could hear something. I even wondered if you were trying to talk to me, Lottie. Then I worked out where you were."

Lottie stood up, and Sofie bounced up the steps towards Ariadne's flat. "We came to see you," she told Ariadne. "Lottie needs to talk to you."

"We both do," Lottie said firmly. "No going and fighting with Tabitha and Shadow; this is too important."

Sofie's ears suddenly drooped. "Shadow is – not here," she whispered.

Lottie froze, one foot lifted above a step, and

stared at Ariadne. Surely she would have told her if Shadow had gone?

She shook her head. "He is, Sofie, but he's very tired. He's not talking." She sighed, and then smiled. "Not even to tell Tabitha off."

"Are you all right?" Lottie asked Ariadne worriedly. She'd had Shadow for ever.

Ariadne nodded, but she didn't look all right. She was always pale, but usually her black clothes suited her. Today she looked as though she was wrapped up in them for warmth, and that was all.

"We'll go." Lottie half-turned to go back down the stairs, but Sofie barked after her sharply. "Lottie, no! You must talk to Ariadne. I cannot tell you properly, it means too much to me. You need someone to talk to. We need her. And even Tabitha, if she can be not rude for a little while."

Ariadne raised her eyebrows. "It's serious, then?" she asked with a tiny smile, which faded when she saw the look on Lottie's face when she turned to go back up the stairs. "Oh, Lottie, I'm sorry. My mind's full of Shadow, and I'm not thinking. Come on." She swept Lottie into the flat with an arm around her shoulders and pushed her gently into a chair, while she fussed around making hot chocolate, offering cocoa powder and marshmallows, anything to keep up a soft, soothing chatter, to take the lost look out of Lottie's eyes.

"Don't put anything special in it," Lottie muttered, rather ungraciously. "I need to be able to think."

"So you don't want an extra square of chocolate in the bottom then?" Ariadne asked her, fingers poised over the mug.

"Oh, all right then. You knew what I meant." Lottie smiled reluctantly. "Where's Shadow, Ariadne?"

"On my bed," Ariadne answered, deliberately turning away and pretending she was looking for the sugar. Tabitha rubbed against her side, lovingly, and Ariadne gave her a lick of the cream.

Lottie saw that she was distracting herself, and didn't say anything.

Ariadne turned back, and they smiled at each other, in a grateful conspiracy to leave the subject alone. She put the chocolate mugs on the table and slid gracefully into her chair. "So. Tell me why you were lurking on my stairs."

Lottie sipped her hot chocolate. It was the perfect temperature. It was one of those useful bits of magic that Ariadne was amazingly good at, and

Pandora would never bother with because she would think it was beneath her. That thought helped. She smiled lovingly at Ariadne. She didn't want to be anyone else's apprentice.

"Pandora grabbed me on the way home from school," she began, but Ariadne jumped up and ran round the table so quickly that she didn't run at all, she was just *there*.

"What did she do?" Ariadne snapped. "Did she hurt you? I've had enough of this, I'm going to—" She stopped short of saying "kill her" but Lottie knew she wanted to. And she meant it. It wasn't like Danny shouting it through their bedroom wall after she let Sofie eat his last hoarded Mars bar.

Lottie had a feeling that Ariadne might not take this well. She was usually so calm. But then, Sofie gave Lottie a great deal of feisty confidence. What if it was Shadow who'd kept Ariadne gentle? What would she be like with only Tabitha? Probably bouncier. Lottie tried not to giggle.

Ariadne eyed her thoughtfully, one hand cupping Lottie's cheek. "Well, you still look like you. And even though I can't get in your head, you *feel* like you too."

Lottie stared into Ariadne's moss-green eyes, and let down all her barriers. Sofie made a strange little noise of surprise, and Lottie flashed her an apologetic look. She brought the encounter with Pandora to the front of her mind, and watched Ariadne while she learned it – and all Lottie's thoughts and worries and unmade decisions.

Ariadne pulled her hand away and sat down on the floor – or collapsed, rather, with her legs tucked under her. Tabitha climbed into her lap, nuzzling her. "You can't," Ariadne said flatly. "You mustn't." She gazed up at Lottie. "Not just because I would miss you so much. You can't give yourself to Pandora, Lottie. It would be like handing a madman a gun." She rubbed her hands over her face, shivering. "I haven't felt you like that for a while – since I taught you to keep proper guards up. Lottie, you're so *strong*. I don't know if it's Tom coming back, or the efforts you and Sofie have made to try and help him, but your power's bubbling over in you. Give that to Pandora – I can't imagine what she'd do."

"But she can mend my dad," Lottie said pleadingly. "I can't do it right, Ariadne. I don't want to be her apprentice. I don't know what she'd do to me, and I think she'd probably kill Sofie. Oh, you know it too!" she told Sofie almost angrily, when she felt the little dog's shock. "She'd never stand for you answering back, and you couldn't stop. But if I say no, how can I tell my dad I gave up the chance to bring his mind back?"

"Lottie, I know Tom. I knew him really well, when he was here before, and I was friends with Jack and your aunt. He would rather die than let you do this. How do you think he would feel, having all his memories back, knowing exactly how he left you and your mum, and then seeing what he'd done to you now? That he'd been the way for Pandora to get her claws into you?"

Lottie stared miserably into her hot chocolate, still magically hot. "I just don't think I can go back to the shop and see him. Not knowing I'm doing this."

"Believe that he would want it this way," Ariadne told her, her voice thrumming with power.

"He said so, Lottie," Sofie reminded her. "Remember him shaking you, after Pandora touched you? He was in a panic that she might have hurt you."

Lottie nodded, suddenly looking up with clear eyes. "She offered to bring his mind back, and he said no, didn't he? He said he didn't want her version of everything, the bits of his memory she'd picked out." She shook her head. "I'd forgotten that somehow."

"You see?" Ariadne nodded. "Don't let her convince you, Lottie. She'll try again; she'd already wafted away some of the memories you needed. You wouldn't be doing Tom a favour, giving him over to her. If he let her in his mind again, he'd probably never get her out."

Lottie knew it was the right answer, but it didn't make her feel any better. She crept into the shop like a thief, and she was silent all the way through tea. Even Sofie delicately picking the unknown shellfish out of Uncle Jack's interesting seafood pasta didn't make her laugh.

"What's up with you?" Danny whispered, nudging her. Septimus, his black rat, was on his shoulder. He'd refused to eat the pasta, and was nibbling a mint toffee and watching her inquisitively.

"I'll tell you later," Lottie promised, pushing the pasta around her plate. "What's the matter with my dad?" she asked, suddenly realizing that he was doing the same thing.

"Your mum phoned. She thought he was *my*

dad," Danny muttered. "Think it got to him a bit; he dropped the phone and went out and he hasn't said much since."

Lottie gulped, tears suddenly burning her eyes. It was all so *unfair*.

"Lottie, can you help me with the washing up?" her uncle asked her, after they'd all picked at their food enough.

Lottie nodded cautiously, sensing that this wasn't just about her turn to help out.

"Your mum phoned," Uncle Jack explained, once Danny and her dad had disappeared. Danny was trying to get his newfound uncle into football, since Uncle Jack wasn't the slightest bit interested, and even though he tried, his idiotic comments only made Danny furious.

"I hadn't realized she wanted you to go back to your old house." He didn't say it critically, but Lottie knew she should have told him.

"Sorry," she said quietly, rubbing over and over again at an already dry plate.

"What are you going to do?"

"I'm not going back!" Lottie looked up at him sharply, and felt Sofie staring at him too. "You won't make me, will you?"

"Of course not," her uncle sighed. "But I think

you're going to have to tell her the truth. She sounded very hurt on the phone."

Lottie put the plate away in the cupboard, and picked up another. "If I tell her now, when she's already upset, I don't think she'll believe me. I think it would be better to show her. But I don't know how to get her back here. Did she say anything about our flat?"

"Mm-hm. Apparently it's still let out to someone, and they've asked for a bit more time to pack their things up. She wanted to know if she could come and stay here in a couple of weeks. I said yes, of course. I couldn't think of a good reason why not. And she's going to have to find out about your dad some time."

"He doesn't want her to see him the way he is," Lottie protested.

Her uncle handed her a mug to dry. "Then you'd better hurry up and get his memory back, hadn't you?" He gave her a stern look. "And I've spoken to Ariadne, and I don't mean by giving yourself up to Pandora in some stupid, dangerous bargain, Lottie Grace. I don't how you could even consider it."

"Thanks, Ariadne," Lottie muttered, but she was smiling.

*

Lottie wandered slowly back through the shop to find Horace. She had a feeling that the strange bird knew more about her father than he was telling.

The old parrot was asleep on his perch in the window with his head tucked half under his wing, and Lottie sighed quietly and started to turn away.

"What is it, girl?" Horace muttered crossly, unhunching himself slightly. "Good Lord, when will you creatures ever learn to move quietly? Billions of years of evolution, and you still sound like elephants."

"Elephants, they also have had many years of evolution," Sofie pointed out, but Horace only glared at her.

"Are you all right, Horace?" Lottie asked. The parrot quite often did a crossword with Uncle Jack in the evening, and since her father had come back the three of them had spent a lot of time talking together. So it seemed strange that Horace was half-asleep.

"My feathers are itching. Oh, not literally," he added, seeing Lottie start to scan the shelves for some sort of parrot tonic. "No room for metaphor in this place. You humans would call it itchy feet." He nibbled irritably at his fluffed-out feathers, then stretched out his neck, twisting as though it was uncomfortable.

"You want to go away?" Sofie asked. She sounded unflatteringly hopeful, and Horace leered at her.

"No, you fussy little badger-hunter. Not yet, anyway." He stretched out one knobbly grey foot and considered it carefully. "I need to change. I can feel it coming on. I keep seeing sparkles in all the dark corners, and my feathers feel frazzled. I want to flame up! So right now I have to conserve my energy." He looked sideways at Lottie with one bright yellow eye. "Lottie, dearest, that was a tactful way of asking you to go away because I need to sleep. Tact does not appear to be working. Go away." He turned his back on them pointedly.

"The rudeness!" Sofie grumbled as they headed upstairs. "Really, he is not at all agreeable."

7

Lottie suddenly sat bolt upright in bed. It was very dark, and she had no idea what time it was. "Sofie! Are you there?" she whispered sharply.

"Mmm. What is that strange noise?" Sofie sounded spooked too, which made Lottie feel even worse.

Lottie's door swung open with a bang, and she screamed. Sofie stood up on Lottie's stomach, barking, all the fur standing up along her spine.

"Sofie, shut up!" Danny snapped. "Lottie, I'm trying to sleep, will you stop making weird noises! It's past midnight and I've got to get up in the morning and do my science homework!"

"It isn't me," Lottie gasped. "It's coming from downstairs, I think. We have to go downstairs."

"I don't, I'm going back to bed," Danny told her crossly, but he followed her, all the same, as she padded across the landing carrying Sofie.

The strange noises grew louder as they stood at the top of the stairs, like a kind of eerie music. Lottie set her feet on the steps without thinking and half-floated down the stairs, not feeling them under her bare feet. The music carried her down, drawing her into the shop.

Her dad and Uncle Jack were already there, and all the animals were awake, gathered on the edges of their shelves, staring wide-eyed at the window. Horace was still on his perch, where Lottie had last seen him, but he was hardly recognizable now. Instead he was a bird-creature made of golden light, his feathers quivering like dancing flames. The burning flame-feathers lit the shop with an eerie brightness, which made all the animals' eyes shine out, so that the shelves were filled with tiny glowing fires.

"What's he doing?" Lottie whispered, drawing closer to her father. He hugged her in to him, and darted her a quick smile before turning back to stare at Horace. "He's changing," he whispered back. "Transforming. Phoenixes burn themselves up like this, then a new phoenix is born out of the ashes of the old. Horace was a raven the last time, before he became a parrot. He's been a magpie, and a sparrow – he didn't keep that form long; he likes to be big."

"What will he be now, do you think?"

"I suspect an owl. He seemed to like it when he tried it out the other day."

"He's going to have to be very careful," Uncle Jack said worriedly. "His hunting instincts will be so strong."

Several of the mice shuffled closer together, and Danny put a protective hand over Septimus, but Sep wriggled away to sit daringly on Danny's shoulder. "Dear boy, if that overgrown torch tries anything with me, I will have no hesitation in attacking him with a fire extinguisher. Don't *fuss*." But he flicked his handsome black whiskers down Danny's cheek in a rat-kiss as he said it.

All at once the glowing creature exploded into a massive ball of flames, and everyone automatically stepped back, even though the fire was strangely heatless.

"Doesn't it hurt him?" Lottie asked worriedly.

Her father shook his head. "I don't think so. I tried to ask him about it – I had a feeling this was coming. But he didn't seem to remember it very clearly."

"I'm not surprised," Danny said, watching the flames shooting up towards the ceiling. "Um, Dad, have we got automatic sprinklers in here?"

"Yes. . ." His father looked up worriedly. "That stupid man from the council said we had to. But I think it's smoke that sets them off. I hope, anyway. I should think a sudden shower of cold water might be a bad idea in the middle of a phoenix rebirth." He dived suddenly behind the counter, popping out a minute later with a pleased expression and a pink flowery umbrella, which he proceeded to open and hold over the burning ball which was Horace. "There! That lady from down the road with the badly behaved Siamese left it yesterday."

"What about me?" Sofie asked plaintively. "I do not like to get wet. Oh, very well," she added crossly when everyone except Lottie glared at her. "I suppose I will manage. But you will be sorry if I catch a chill."

Danny grinned at Lottie. "You know, your familiar's meant to reflect your personality," he whispered.

"Yes," Lottie hissed back. "Which is why Sep's

unbelievably lazy and lives on sweets. Shut up."

The flames were towering higher and higher, so that Uncle Jack was having to stand on tiptoe to keep the umbrella over the top. "Do phoenix-flames set fire to things?" he asked his brother, looking worried.

"Not usually. But then I shouldn't think many people have held an umbrella over one. Put it down, Jack. The sprinklers aren't going off, and I think Horace could cope with it anyway. Ah, look!"

The flames suddenly died back, leaving a pile of silvery ashes, which settled for a second, then reformed into the most unbelievably bright silver-white shape – like the afterglow from staring at the sun. Everyone blinked, and then the shape cracked open like the egg it was, and a tiny flame-creature uncurled itself inside.

It grew incredibly fast, still golden-red and eye-burning to look at, till it was the size of some large bird, like a peacock. It had long, trailing tail feathers, which glittered like some kind of expensive jewelled brooch. At last it seemed to settle on Horace's dingy old wooden perch, its scarlet claws clicking as it sidestepped along the wood, and it peered out at its audience with one bright yellow eye.

Lottie smiled. It was still Horace after all – that same yellow-eyed glare.

The phoenix fluttered his tail feathers and took an enormous leap into the air, swooping out over their heads, flame-feathers streaming behind him, glimmering in every shade of red and orange and gold.

With a delighted squeak, Fred leaped out from his shelf, seizing the phoenix's tail and riding along on it like a small pink surfer.

"Fred!" Uncle Jack yelled. "Get off! Jump! He'll burn you up, jump now!" Fred looked down at his smoking claws and threw himself over the side of the sparkling tail, landing in Uncle Jack's outstretched hands. "Ooohh, that was the best!" he chirruped. "How many mice have done that?" Then he fell over backwards in Uncle Jack's hand, his whiskers fizzling at the ends.

"Watch!" Lottie's dad nudged her, and she looked back up at the sparkling bird. His feathers were changing now, the wings darkening to crimson, like a cooling fire settling down to embers. "He's starting to change. He'll drop the wish-feather soon."

"They do grant wishes, then?" Lottie asked, a sudden hope growing in her heart.

"If you're lucky enough to catch it. He'll want to go higher; we'd better open the back door." He darted out into the kitchen and flung the door open wide for Horace, who burst out with a delighted scream, shooting up into the black night and trailing a shower of golden-red sparks like a winged comet.

"Everyone'll be complaining that we missed fireworks night," Danny said, grinning.

"Look!" Sofie struggled in Lottie's arms, staring up into the sky. "A feather!"

She was right – a glowing golden feather was spiralling slowly down towards them, its gold-white heat cooling to glittering metal as it fell into Lottie's outstretched hand. It felt softly warm and magically alive, burning only with its power now.

"Wish!" Lottie's father urged her, smiling, and Lottie closed her eyes.

But what to wish for? There were so many things.

Never to have to leave Sofie behind.

Her mother to come home and understand the magic after all, so she'd never want to make Lottie leave. Then she'd love Lottie's father again, so Lottie could have a fairy-tale family.

And if her father remembered them all, if he remembered everything, then he could fight to bring her mother back again, and it would all be perfect. Wouldn't it? Except, then her mother would be in Netherbridge, and so would Pandora, and somehow that didn't seem like a very good idea. Lottie shook her head worriedly, trying to puzzle it out. If only she'd had longer to think! She could have planned it all out, done all the clever things one was supposed to do with genies, about wishing for more wishes, though she had a feeling Horace might tell her not to be greedy and peck her ear off if she tried that!

"Hurry, Lottie, it is fading away!" Sofie told her, sniffing the golden magic and sneezing.

Bring Dad's memory back, Horace. Please. That's my wish.

Lottie felt the feather burn with a rush of fiery magic, as the wish surged through her. Then she sat down on the cold stone floor of the yard, clutching a cold metal feather. She looked up with streaming eyes as Horace swirled towards her, the fiery golden shape cooling now, and settling into the brown and cream feathers of an enormous owl, still with those yellow eyes. Now the eyes were huge and round, with night-black pupils, and they entranced Lottie as Horace settled on her father's shoulder and leaned down close to talk to her.

"It's done. Tell no one. It will happen." He blinked slowly. "But I warn you, Lottie. Wishes can be deceitful things. You may not like the way it comes about."

8

Lottie wasn't sure what Horace's warning had meant. She was just waiting for her wish to come true. Everyone else very carefully didn't ask her what she had wished for, except for Fred, who was desperate to know, and most upset that he had missed the wish-feather by being unconscious. He seemed convinced that if he had been awake, he would have been the one to catch it, and he would have wished for a lifetime supply of raisins and coffee sugar.

Lottie kept looking at her father, hoping that he would suddenly smile and stare at her as a flood of memories swept into his mind, but it wasn't happening.

"Lottie, what's the matter?" her dad asked her a couple of days later, as they cleaned out Henrietta's cage together. Henrietta was currently living with a small boy who Uncle Jack was sure pulled the legs off things. If he tried it with Henrietta, he would get a nasty shock.

Lottie gazed at Henrietta's fresh wood shavings, as though they might give her a useful answer.

"You keep looking at me as though you're waiting for something. Have I missed something? It's not your birthday, is it?" he asked, in a horrified voice.

Lottie smiled at him. "No. But it is my birthday at the end of this month," she added. She was fairly sure Uncle Jack would tell him, but that relied on Uncle Jack remembering himself, and seeing as he'd almost forgotten Danny's birthday, it was probably best to be on the safe side.

"So, what is it?"

"She is worrying about her wish," Horace told him smugly, clashing his claws on the cage bars. He had kept up his worrying habit of walking on top of the mice cages and staring into them. It had been bad enough when he was a parrot, but now that he was an owl, several of the mice had given Uncle Jack notice. They said it was against the terms of their contract to be terrorized, and couldn't be persuaded that they didn't actually have a contract. Lottie blamed Fred, for watching far too much television.

"Don't do that," Lottie's dad said, gently persuading Horace on to his arm. "You're only doing it to tease."

"I am rather hungry," Horace said hopefully, bending his neck round at a strange owl angle to look pleadingly at Lottie's dad. "Really quite terribly hungry. Would you have any of those delicious sticky snacks?"

Horace had developed a fondness for Uncle Jack's special lizard treats, which were black and gooey and had bits sticking out of them that Lottie didn't want to think about, bearing in mind that lizards mostly lived on insects.

Her dad frowned. "One. And then you'll have to wait till you go out later. It's nearly dark. And for heaven's sake, don't bring dinner back here this time. I thought the mice were going to demand we hold a wake yesterday, and Fred and Peach have still got those black ribbons tied round their tails."

Horace sniggered. Lottie was sure he'd done it on purpose; he'd always loved upsetting the mice.

"Don't worry, Lottie," he told her, with some difficulty, as the lizard treat was gluing his beak together. "Like I told you, the wish will come true soon enough."

Lottie shivered. Horace's yellow eyes looked almost wicked in some lights, and she wasn't sure how much she trusted him.

"Leave her alone." Sofie came bouncing down the stairs – she had been asleep on Lottie's bed.

Horace flew down to the back of a chair to be closer to her. "We're only talking, Sofie," he chuckled. "Lottie and I are interested in the progress of her wish, that's all."

Sofie growled irritably at him. "Lottie, I have just woken up, and I need coffee; make me some. Please. He irritates me, that one," she added quietly as they went into the kitchen. "He likes to tease me."

"Me too," Lottie agreed. "I wish he'd just get on and grant that wish, but maybe it isn't all that simple. I keep wondering if Pandora's going to turn up asking if I want to agree to her bargain."

Sofie nodded, sniffing happily at the coffee tin. "Mmf. We said we would go back." Then she jumped down off the chair she'd been standing on, looking back up at Lottie in horror. "She is coming, Lottie! She is evil, that one; did she hear us talking?"

"Now?" Lottie yelped aloud, jumping up. "Pandora's coming?"

"Now," Sofie agreed. "She is coming to the shop."

Lottie flung herself to the door. Somehow it seemed incredibly important to be there waiting for Pandora, like having a defence prepared, however feeble it really was. Sofie galloped after her, ears flapping, and Lottie's dad looked up in surprise as they skidded into the shop.

"She's coming," Lottie gasped, staring at the door, and her dad didn't bother to ask who. He dropped the newspaper and stood up, Horace on his shoulder, swivelling his great owl eyes from side to side.

Pandora laughed as she opened the door and saw them all there waiting for her. "How lovely," she cooed. "All of you lined up. A little welcoming committee."

Sofie hissed, and very carefully did not shrink back when Pandora turned to glare at her. Lottie could feel her shivering, but Sofie refused to look away.

"When you are my apprentice, Lottie, that little dog will have to learn some manners." Pandora murmered. She was still smiling, but her voice was cold.

Sofie looked up at Lottie, her eyes round with fear, and Lottie clung to her tightly. It was exactly as she had said it would be. Even if she had not been able to wish for her father to get his memory back, Lottie could not have condemned herself and Sofie to life with Pandora – Sofie's life wouldn't have lasted very long anyway.

Sending reassuring thoughts of love to Sofie, Lottie looked up at Pandora, noticing that she was unhealthily pale. Lottie remembered the confrontation she'd had with Pandora a few weeks before, where the enchantress had told her that she could reach inside her chest and stop her heart. She had almost believed her. It was all about what you thought was true, and frightening her had been what Pandora wanted. But it worked both ways. If she acted scared, she would be scared. If she didn't let her heart thump in her chest, she would be calm. Lottie smiled back at Pandora as sweetly as she could.

"So. Lottie. I thought you were coming back to talk to me?" Pandora asked, leaning lazily against the counter and fluttering her eyelashes at Lottie's dad.

Lottie nodded. "Yes. I was still thinking."

"And have you thought, now?" Pandora raised her eyebrows.

Lottie looked over at her dad quickly. She hadn't felt she could bear to tell him about Pandora's offer, and she didn't think Uncle Jack had either. So he had no idea what Pandora was talking about.

Unfortunately, Pandora intercepted that quick glance. "You haven't told him, have you, Lottie?" she purred.

"Told me what?" Lottie's father snapped.

Pandora held out a hand to Lottie, as though she expected her to take it. "Lottie," her voice dripped with mock-concern, "I do think this is something you should tell your father yourself. After all, he should know what it is you're doing for him, don't you think? You should give him the chance to be grateful." She shot a strange look at Tom. It was half loving, half spiteful, as though Pandora herself was torn between the two.

"He doesn't need to be. . ." Lottie muttered, turning red.

Pandora nodded. "Of course. You're right, Lottie. He shouldn't need to thank you – it's no more than any loving daughter would do."

"What is going on?" Lottie's dad's voice rose, and Horace opened out his great wings and beat them fiercely, letting out an eerie screech.

Lottie was sure Pandora knew she was going to

say no. She was just trying to bump up Lottie's guilt as much as possible. Unfortunately, it was working.

She's trying to make you unhappy, so you cannot think to fight, Sofie whispered in Lottie's mind.

Fight? Lottie knew she sounded panicky, but she couldn't help it.

Yes. Why else would she come here? She knows you are going to say no. Look at her. She is angry, and she has come to fight.

Lottie stood up straighter, drawing strength from Sofie's velvet fur. "I won't do it," she said, trying not to let her voice shake. She almost managed it.

Pandora raised her eyebrows. "Lottie! You mean you're going to condemn your father to living without his memories?" she asked in a shocked voice.

Lottie stared her down. "No. You are."

Do not tell her about the wish, Sofie said urgently. *I do not know why – but it is important. Do not tell her.*

Lottie shook her head a fraction. She was sure Sofie was right. It was too important a secret to share. She had a feeling that if she told anyone, the wish wouldn't work.

Good girl, Lottie. The voice in her mind wasn't Sofie's. It was low, and hooting. Horace. Lottie glanced over at him in shock, and found the owl staring at her with those hypnotic yellow eyes. *The wish has linked us,* he explained. *Do not let her distract you with these silly mind games, Lottie. Protect Tom. He's still weaker than he should be, without his memories of magic. Fight for him – again.*

Lottie nodded.

"Oh, Tom." Pandora shook her head. "I'm so sorry. I was sure that Lottie would do this for you. Such a little thing."

Lottie's father put both hands flat on the counter and leaned over it. Lottie blinked, almost sure she could see a strange silvery shadow around him, flowing and changing, like a second Tom. She swallowed, her mouth suddenly dry. How strong was her father's magic? And did he know about it all? Could he control it?

He spoke, very slowly and steadily. "Lottie is my daughter. I may not remember her, but I love her. I would rather die than have her involved with you in any way. I don't know what you've asked her to do, and I don't care. She won't do it."

Pandora's fingers clenched into her palms, and she hissed furiously as she spoke. "Are you sure you want to do this? Now? Do you really think you can fight with me, in your state?" She laughed angrily, but there were sharp red spots on her cheeks, and her breathing was fast.

Anger, you see? Sofie pointed out, quickly licking Lottie's cheek. *Your father may be weakened like Horace said, but he is so calm. He is still very strong, that one.*

Lottie stroked her, as much for her own comfort as Sofie's. She was trying to stay calm, but she was frightened, far more frightened than she'd been when it was only her facing Pandora. She couldn't lose her father again, not now. She'd only just got him back! She wished Uncle Jack were here to help, Danny too.

You have all of us. It was Sofie's voice, but not just Sofie. Horace's hooting tone was there, and the squeaky little voices of the mice. Every creature in the shop. As Lottie's father walked round the counter to stand face to face with Pandora, gently handing Horace off his shoulder on to his perch, Lottie glanced behind her at the rows of cages.

When Pandora first came to the shop, all the animals had hidden, desperate to stay away from her. Only the warlike hamster Giles had not been terrified of the evilness that seemed to seep out of her like sweat.

Now they were all there, clinging to the bars to

stop themselves from running and hiding under their bedding.

We'll protect you, Lottie! Fred squeaked. He and Peach had their tails knotted together for comfort, and Lottie could see that they had tied them through the bars too. They couldn't run away – however much they wanted to.

Thank you! she whispered lovingly to the tiny mice, and then she looked back at the two people in the middle of the room.

Suddenly, almost faster than she could see, Pandora swept round and flicked her hair across Lottie's dad's face.

It was as though he'd been hit with some poisonous weapon. He reeled away, coughing and wiping at the corner of his mouth. His hand was red, and Lottie gasped as she saw a trickle of blood run down his chin.

But he fought back – standing completely still, with even his eyes closed. Lottie could feel his power as he slung it so gracefully across the room at Pandora, as though it were effortless.

She swayed, the red spots on her cheeks darkening, her white-blonde hair losing some of its eerie glow. But then she straightened up, her face strong and proud.

Lottie's father opened his eyes again, his breathing heavy, and they stared at each other, waiting.

It drained him. They're almost evenly matched, Sofie murmured, watching closely.

Can he beat her? Lottie asked.

I do not know, Lottie.

They did it again. And again. Great bursts of magic, flying across the room, fizzing around in the air, making everything taste strange and sharp. They were both weakening. Lottie's father was starting to tremble.

"Look, I've got pinker," Lottie heard Fred say in a pleased voice. It was true. The heavy swirls of magic were strengthening all the animals. Sofie's fur was sleek and shiny, and her eyes sparkled. *Can't we join in the fight?* she asked Lottie. *I am sure I could bite that Pandora now. I feel* magnifique.

Lottie was never sure if Pandora heard Sofie's thought somehow, or whether she had intended to do it all along. Quite suddenly, she broke off that strange, tense battle with Lottie's father and swung round, focusing all her magic on Lottie instead.

There was nothing for Lottie. No Sofie, no magic, no family. Just a thing that was lost, and didn't even know what it was.

The thing that had been Lottie turned this way and that, desperately searching for *something*, though it didn't know what.

Then at last, there was fur.

Soft fur, wrapped around her, warming her, loving her.

Lottie knew she was Lottie again.

She opened her eyes, painfully, the light beating against them, and gasped with relief at being back.

Sofie was standing on her chest, and every other animal in the shop was curled against her, lending her all their magic to survive.

"You didn't reckon on the animals, did you?" Lottie's father said, his voice hoarse and shaky. "They're loyal to Lottie. Is anyone that loyal to you, Pandora?" Then he froze, as she flung herself at him, blazing with rage.

"Dad!" Lottie yelled, trying to struggle to her feet, but Horace was there first. He swooped from his perch, screaming a battle cry, and tangled his claws in all that shining, magical hair, stabbing furiously with his hooked and dagger-like beak.

Pandora fell back howling, and clutched at Horace, her fingers sparkling with silvery magic.

Horace exploded. There was no other word for it.

It was like the final fire of his transformation, but all in a second – and then there was nothing but floating grey ash, settling snow-like on Pandora, and adding a sickly greyish cast to her face.

"Oh, Horace, no!" Lottie whispered. She couldn't believe he was gone.

"Lottie!" Sofie snapped. "Look!"

Lottie had been watching Pandora wipe away the ashy dust that had streaked across her face; she hadn't seen her father standing by Horace's perch, a handful of the dusty ashes falling through his fingers, staring at Pandora with a face that looked like stone.

"That shadow," Lottie whispered. It was all around him now, a silver halo, and as he walked towards Pandora his footsteps seemed to echo.

"He has found all his magic," Sofie muttered. "Perhaps the anger has brought it back? I do not know. But she had better watch out."

It was a whole different fight. This new, angry Tom simply flung Pandora back against the counter, hardly even needing to touch her, and held her there.

"Because my daughter is watching, I won't hurt you. But I want to. And if you come back here again, believe me, I will."

Pandora summoned up a sickly smile. "I don't have to be here," she hissed, her teeth shining white against the ashy skin. "I can fight you wherever I am. You'll see."

Then she was gone, leaving just a cloud of drifting ash behind.

Lottie stood up shakily. "I'm sorry," she told her dad.

Her father smiled, and gently ran a hand down Sofie's back. "You don't have anything to be sorry for." He looked at Lottie, as though he was seeing her for the first time. "You've grown."

Lottie blinked at him, and Sofie wriggled round to stare.

"Though I suppose I should have expected that, after eight years away."

"You remember!" Lottie rubbed her hand across her eyes. "Oh, Horace. He did it."

"Was that the wish?" her father asked, staring at his dusty palms, and Lottie nodded, stroking a tear-wet finger across the gritty dust.

"It's hot," she murmured sadly, and then she looked up sharply at her father. They stared around the shop as the ashes rose and glittered, hanging in the air like a silvery mist. A mist which coiled and swirled into long feathery shapes, twisting and spinning till a smoky bird streaked above their heads.

"What on earth are you crying for?" Horace looked like a silvery dream-creature, but his voice was exactly the same. "Phoenixes are immortal, Lottie. Good gracious, girl, do you know nothing?" There was a shimmering, and a twitching, and he was an owl again, sitting on her father's shoulder and reaching almost to his ear.

Lottie giggled, and Horace's feathery eyebrows drew together. "I had to expend a certain amount of magical energy," he told her frostily, shifting from claw to tiny claw. "I will be a pygmy owl for a little while."

Sofie snorted. "He is very cute, Lottie, do you not think?"

"It will come back, and I will be large again, and woe betide you then, you nasty, snappish little brute." Horace clacked his beak at Sofie, but she couldn't stop snorting and muttering, "Little! He says little! *Petite chouette!*"

Lottie looked up at her father, and blushed – he was still staring at her, as though he was trying to fit his memories of his tiny daughter on to the new Lottie.

"Do you remember everything?" Lottie asked shyly. It felt like meeting him all over again.

"I think so." Her father scratched the still hissing, fussing Horace under the chin with one finger. "Horace gave us a new start," he murmured.

Lottie nodded. She had thought that when her father recovered, she would want to ask him so many things. But it didn't seem to matter just now.

There was time.

HOLLY WEBB is the author of the bestselling
Lost in the Snow and its sequel, *Lost in the
Storm*, as well as the popular Triplets series.
She has always loved cats and now
owns a very spoilt one.

Have you read Lottie's first adventures?

Catmagic

HOLLY WEBB

1

I am not looking, I am not looking.

Lottie glared straight ahead, ignoring her mother, who was waving determinedly at her through the train window.

Lottie had hardly spoken to her since she'd broken the news two days ago. She was too angry – and if they discussed it, talked it all through, it would be real. Until just about now, Lottie had been convinced that somehow her mum's new job in Paris wasn't really going to happen, that if Lottie really hated the idea, her mum wouldn't go through with it. But it was getting too late to turn back now.

She wasn't going to see her mum all summer and they hadn't even properly said goodbye! Lottie turned suddenly, pressing her hand against the window.

Her mum wasn't there.

The train had already started, and all Lottie could see were strange faces gliding by. She turned right round in her seat, panicking. She didn't even know when she'd see Mum again! Peering frantically out of the corner of the window as the train curved out of the platform, she could see her mum's pink coat. She was still waving. Lottie waved back until the train was right out of the station. Then she sat down again, feeling shaky and sick, and very alone.

A crackly voice over the speaker announced the stations, loads of them, with Netherbridge Halt buried somewhere in the middle. All at once Lottie stopped feeling miserable and went back to being just plain cross. Netherbridge was a tiny little town in the depths of the country somewhere, and Mum was dumping her there. In fact, she wasn't even taking the time to dump Lottie in person, she was just putting her on the train, and leaving her uncle Jack to pick her up at the other end.

"I can't even remember what he looks like," Lottie muttered crossly to herself, blinking back tears. She had met him before, but it was ages ago, at a family party that her mum hadn't really wanted to go to. Lottie's mum didn't like being around Lottie's dad's family any more. She said it made her feel too sad.

Uncle Jack was Lottie's dad's older brother, and he ran a pet shop in Netherbridge. Lottie had never been there, but she'd seen it in the photos Uncle Jack sent every year in his Christmas card. She had one, actually, in her bag. Mum had given it to her, so she would recognize Uncle Jack at the station.

She rummaged through her bag, at last finding the photo wedged inside her book.

Uncle Jack looked very like the photos of Lottie's father. He had the same curly black hair that Lottie had inherited, and very dark eyes. Usually that would have fascinated her, but right now Lottie was less interested in her uncle than the shop behind him – where she was going to be living for the summer. Her mood lifted slightly. Lottie's mum had always been anti-pet, very much so. She said animals were messy and smelly, and wouldn't fit in a flat. Even goldfish, which Lottie didn't think was very reasonable. It would be fun to be around some animals for once – it didn't look like Uncle Jack's was the boring sort of pet shop that only sold collars and cat toys. She peered carefully at the photo. It was hard to see much, but there seemed to be a parrot on a perch in the window, as well as the bags of pet foods. The sign above the shop said Grace's Pet Shop, and there was something else written underneath, but it was too small in the photo to see.

Grace's Pet Shop. It was quite nice to be going somewhere that had her own name written up above the door. Of course, it would have, Uncle Jack being her dad's brother. Lottie leaned back in her seat, staring dreamily out of the window, and wondering what sort of animals the pet shop might have. Kittens, maybe? A small knot of excitement began to grow inside her – not that she was anywhere close to being happy about all this, of course not. She was furious. But there was no point in being so angry she didn't get to enjoy herself at all. It wasn't as if her mum would be around to see whether she was happy or not. Whenever she phoned, Lottie could quite easily be miserable.

Lottie was rather silent in the van on the way back to Uncle Jack's. She'd managed to forget on purpose that Uncle Jack's son, Danny, would be around too – even after Mum kept going on about how nice it would be to get to know her cousin. Danny was only a year older than Lottie was, but he was a lot bigger than her, and extremely good-looking, and he seemed very sure of himself. Not that Lottie was shy, not normally anyway, but it was hard to know what to say to him. Were they supposed to be friends just because they were related? Lottie supposed it was a bit weird for him too, suddenly having a cousin he hardly knew dumped in his house. Danny wasn't unfriendly, but he just gazed out of the window, and didn't talk, which made it even more noticeable that her uncle was trying very hard to keep the conversation going.

Uncle Jack's van smelled weird, Lottie thought, trying not to sniff too obviously. Maybe it was pet food? She jumped suddenly as something cold was pushed against her hand. Uncle Jack heard her gasp and turned round. The van swerved.

"Dad, watch it! You're driving!" Danny yelled.

"Sorry, sorry!" Uncle Jack murmured, waving apologetically at the driver of the car behind who was looking a bit unnerved. "Don't worry, Lottie, it's just Sofie, she was asleep in there, I should have warned you."

Lottie looked down at the pile of blankets she'd thought she was sitting next to. It was wriggling, and now a damp black nose emerged, followed by a pointed muzzle, and a pair of liquid brown eyes. The little dog twitched her ginger eyebrows at Lottie, and lifted the side of her mouth in an unmistakable smile.

Danny looked over his seat, and let out a low whistle. "You're lucky, she likes you."

"How do you know?" Lottie asked, stroking Sofie's nose.

Danny turned back round, grinning. "She hasn't bitten your hand off."

Lottie gave the dog a doubtful look, and then frowned. It almost looked like Sofie had winked at her.

"Now, that's not fair," Uncle Jack disagreed. "All dachshunds are temperamental. Sofie's just choosy about the company she keeps."

"Yeah, tell that to the postman. . ." Danny said, smirking.

"He trod on her!" Uncle Jack said indignantly.

Sofie swarmed her way out of the blankets and coiled herself into Lottie's lap, where she gazed up at her innocently. *Me. . .?* she seemed to be saying. She was a beautiful dog, shiny black, with ginger paws and those amazing ginger eyebrows. She looked as though she'd been polished. She answered one question anyway – it looked as though Lottie would get to spend the holiday with at least one animal.

They parked in a yard behind the pet shop, and went in the back way. Uncle Jack dropped Lottie's bags, and went to turn over the Closed sign on the door, while Lottie looked round in amazement, still hugging Sofie tightly. She'd never imagined anything like this. The shop was in an odd, crooked little house on the high street – Lottie had had a brief glimpse of the front as they drove past. It was black and white, with a big, many-paned bay window that took up the whole of the narrow front. But it seemed somehow to be much larger on the inside, full of corners and alcoves and niches. Every inch was packed with cages and tanks, wedged together all the way up the walls. It was oddly silent, and Lottie had the disconcerting feeling that she was being watched – almost examined. Then she decided she must be imagining things as the shop was filled with the squeak and scuffle of hundreds of tiny creatures.

Uncle Jack turned back from the door, smiling. "Well, here you are, Lottie. Grace's Pet Shop. Otherwise known as the Mouse Emporium!"

2

Lottie sat on her new bed, looking round the bedroom. It was really sweet. It had obviously been a little girl's bedroom sometime before, because it had pink spotty curtains and pale pink walls. The bedclothes had pink spots too. In fact, there was something very weird about those pink spots. Lottie was sure she'd seen them before somewhere. Maybe one of her friends had something similar. Although, to be honest, the whole room felt familiar. She leaned back against the wall, staring round thoughtfully. The room was right at the top of the house, so it had a sloping ceiling, and the window was oddly crooked. No one she knew had a bedroom like this. So why did it feel like she'd been here before?

"Lottie!" Her uncle was yelling up the stairs. "Come and have a drink!"

Lottie gave one last considering look around, shook her head, and went downstairs.

Uncle Jack and Danny were in the shop, sitting on stools by the counter with drinks and biscuits.

"I still think we're never going to get away with it," Danny said, shrugging. "How can we?"

"We just need to be a bit careful, it might not be for long," Uncle Jack told him soothingly, but he looked worried.

"Well, how long is she staying? I don't get it, does her mum just not want her or something—" Then he saw Lottie coming and shut up, shoving a biscuit into his mouth whole instead.

Uncle Jack looked very embarrassed. His ears turned red and he glared at Danny. "Lottie! Tea? Orange juice? Have a biscuit!"

It was obvious they'd been talking about her. Lottie supposed it was only natural, but she couldn't help feeling hurt. Especially because Danny had summed up exactly what she felt. Lottie's mum's exciting career move to Paris was more important than her own daughter. Suddenly she was blinking back tears, and she stared very hard at one of the cages without really looking at what was in it.

"Do you like mice?" Uncle Jack asked hopefully, moving over to her.

"Yes," Lottie sniffed. It wasn't as if she'd ever really known any, but she was sure she did. Blinking again, she realized that the cage she was staring at so hard was full of beautiful little white mice, so tiny and delicate, with ruby-red eyes. They were all looking at her, interestedly. It was quite odd to be stared at by mice.

"A new face," Uncle Jack said, rather hurriedly. "Very curious, mice. Always like to know what's going on. Don't you? Mmmm." He tapped the cage-front affectionately, and the mice skittered off.

Lottie looked round at some of the other cages. "You've got a lot of mice," she said in surprise. Several of the cages held mice, in all different colours. Lottie peered carefully at the topmost cage. Were those mice *pink*?

"Oh, we specialize in mice." Uncle Jack hurriedly steered Lottie to a cageful of beautiful glossy black ones. "We *are* the Mouse Emporium. But we have almost everything else too. Kittens, rats, lizards, goldfinches. We had a scorpion until last week, he was *very* interesting." Uncle Jack looked thoughtful. "He was quite sneaky though, kept getting out of his tank. Bit of a worry."

"Miracle we're still alive," Danny muttered.

Lottie squirmed, feeling suddenly itchy. She hoped none of the other pets were given to escaping. Especially not the small ones, with lots of legs. . .

"Your mum said you liked animals?" Uncle Jack suggested hopefully.

"Oh yes!" Lottie nodded. "Would I be allowed to help in the shop at all?" she asked shyly.

Uncle Jack looked like he wanted to hug her, and

Danny gave a cough that sounded suspiciously like a snigger.

"Of *course* you can." Uncle Jack led her over to a large run, where four black kittens were playing on some tree branches that had been built into a sort of climbing frame. They had loads of toys too. In fact, all the animals in the shop seemed to have toys and lots of things to do. It was also the cleanest pet shop Lottie had ever seen. "Would you mind playing with these?" her uncle asked anxiously. "They need lots of handling, so as to get used to people, and it's one of those jobs that I just don't get time for."

Lottie grinned. She was getting the feeling she was going to enjoy this summer.

Look out for Lottie's other adventures!

HOLLY WEBB

Dogmagic

A TAIL OF ENCHANTMENT!

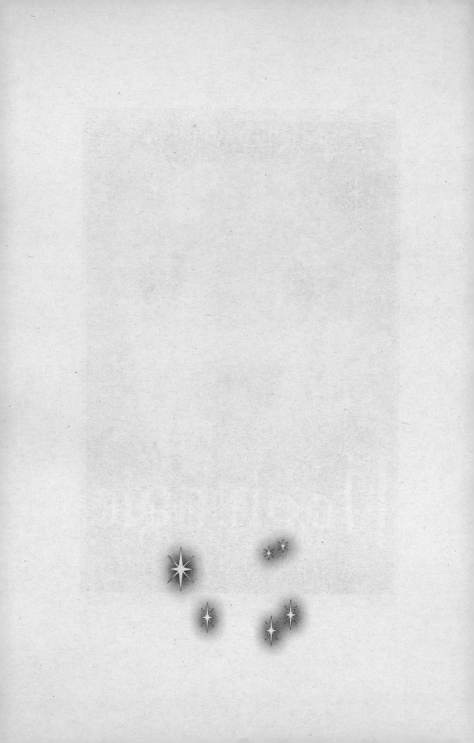

HOLLY WEBB

Hamstermagic

A SPELL~BINDING TAIL

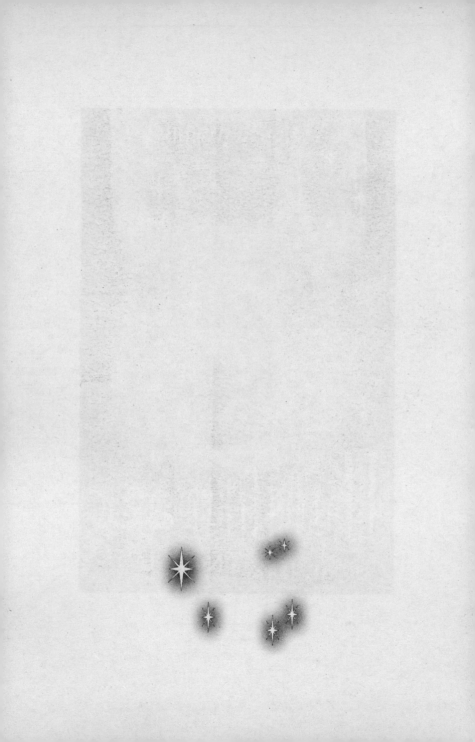